"I need secretarial help," Mitch said.

"Helen," he continued, "my personal assistant, had to leave on a family emergency a few days ago. I've had two incompetent secretaries in since then, and this office is in more chaos than if I hadn't had anyone."

"I have a job waiting for me in Fort Lauderdale," Ginny said.

"I'll make you a deal. I'll make up the difference for Joey's surgery—you can have it done in Dallas. In exchange, you work for me until Helen returns." That would solve the problem of a temp leaving in a huff.

Ginny stared at the man. He would pay for the surgery of a total stranger? *What was the catch?*

Barbara McMahon was born and raised in the South, but settled in California after spending a year flying around the world for an international airline. After settling down to raise a family and work for a computer firm, she began writing when her children started school. Now, feeling fortunate in being able to realize a long-held dream of quitting her "day job" and writing full-time, she and her husband have moved to California's Sierra Nevada, where she finds her desire to write is stronger than ever. With the beauty of the mountains visible from her windows, and the pace of life slower than the hectic San Francisco Bay Area where they previously resided, she finds more time than ever to think up stories and characters and share them with others through writing. Barbara loves to hear from readers. You can reach her at P.O. Box 977, Pioneer, CA 95666-0977, U.S.A. Readers can also contact Barbara at her Web site: www.barbaramcmahon.com

Books by Barbara McMahon

HARLEQUIN ROMANCE®

Don't miss any of our special offers. Write to us at the following address for information on our newest releases.

Harlequin Reader Service
U.S.: 3010 Walden Ave., P.O. Box 1325, Buffalo, NY 14269
Canadian: P.O. Box 609, Fort Erie, Ont. L2A 5X3

THE BOSS'S
CONVENIENT PROPOSAL

Barbara McMahon

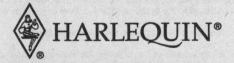

TORONTO • NEW YORK • LONDON
AMSTERDAM • PARIS • SYDNEY • HAMBURG
STOCKHOLM • ATHENS • TOKYO • MILAN • MADRID
PRAGUE • WARSAW • BUDAPEST • AUCKLAND

ISBN 0-373-03785-6

THE BOSS'S CONVENIENT PROPOSAL

First North American Publication 2004.

PROLOGUE

GINNY MORGAN hated spring break. It wasn't only because of the long hours, though for those two weeks every spring her shifts doubled up and days off were only a memory. She was sure half the college students from eastern schools and most of the ones in the Midwest flocked to Fort Lauderdale to party hardy. They came to drink, have fun and fall in love.

It was the best of times because of the extra tips and the exuberant spirits rampant among the visitors.

It was the worst of times because of the memories that surfaced. Memories kept tucked away for most of the year. Only the lingering sadness remained when she looked into her son's eyes.

Ginny wiped the table, stacking glasses and dishes in the bin. Where was that blasted busboy? Honestly, if she were the manager of Tom's Fish Shack, she'd fire Manuel and hire someone more reliable.

Lifting the heavy bin, she carried it into the kitchen and dumped it by the sink. The steam from the simmering pots and soup caldrons made the restaurant's kitchen an instant steam bath. The greasy smell of frying shrimp filled the air. She glanced at the counter, none of her orders were up yet, so she escaped to the relative coolness of the restaurant proper.

Glancing around her assigned area with a practiced eye, Ginny noticed the group of giggling college girls were about to leave. She watched as they laughed among themselves, and threw saucy glances at the boys that wandered into view on the spacious open-air deck. Skimpy swimsuits were the order of the day. And the coverups never did their job, revealing more than concealing.

She'd worn one such over her own bikini five years ago when—

No, she wasn't going to go there again! It had been five years, time to move on beyond the Cinderella story that had an unhappy ending. She was older and far wiser now than she had been then. Never again would she get caught up in the frenzy and romance of spring break. Never listen to lies wrapped in romantic overtones. Nor believe a man when he said he loved her after only two weeks. Maybe never.

Now she was single mother, with a son who gave her more delight than she had a right to. Her life had not taken the path she'd wanted so long ago, but she wouldn't trade Joey for all the tea in China, as her aunt Edith used to say.

Nothing came without a price, however. She smiled at the girls when they waved on their way out, hoping they left a large tip. They'd been extravagant in ordering, then left half the food on the table. Sure enough, they'd been equally lavish in their tips.

Ginny scooped up the money and put it in her pocket. Another few dollars for Joey's surgery fund. Her goal was to save enough to have the operation done before he started school next year. It wasn't right that a little boy should have crossed eyes. She'd done her best to shelter him from cruel insults, but she knew starting school that way would cause unmerciful teasing. She refused to accept that for her son.

But since the surgery was elective rather than life-saving, the meager insurance coverage she had from the restaurant didn't cover the procedure. The full cost would have to be borne by her. And she was still a few thousand dollars short.

Ginny stacked the dishes from the crowded table in another bin, resigned to the fact Manuel had disappeared once again. Taking the discarded newspaper, she folded it and tucked it beneath her arm. She enjoyed reading the newspapers from all over that customers left. Once she'd had dreams of leaving Fort Lauderdale and seeing Atlanta, or Washington, or even New York. But dreams of college and travel had vanished from her horizon when she'd become pregnant with Joey.

She dumped the dishes then served another two tables before time for her break. Reaching for the purloined newspaper, she hurried outside, away from the din and commotion. Sitting beneath a huge old palm, which offered scant shade in the heat of the day, she spread open the paper. It was the *Dallas Tribune*. For a second, her heart clutched. She looked up, glimpsing the blue Atlantic between the souvenir shops and sidewalks crowded with randy college kids. It was as if she looked into the past. Texas. *He* had been from Texas.

Sighing softly, she picked up the paper and began to scan the various articles. She was almost finished with the front section when a small headline on the lower left caught her eye.

John Mitchell Holden and Family Donate One

Million Dollars to the Children's Last Wish Foundation.

Ginny started at the words unable to believe her eyes.

John Mitchell Holden.

Five years vanished immediately and she was once again the young girl who had been swept away by the big brash Texan who had charmed her socks off, overcome her innate inhibitions and seduced her into bed. Two weeks of heaven. The glamor of it, the rush of excitement, the heady delight, the spellbinding glory of those days filled her mind. Her heart raced in memory. She'd been wined and dined in fine fashion. Told over and over she was the prettiest thing he'd ever seen. She could almost hear the echo of that sexy Texas drawl.

Then—he'd vanished without a word. Spring break had ended and he'd returned to Texas.

Ginny had never heard from him again.

She had not known where to contact him. She had poured over telephone books and searched the Internet trying to locate any and every Holden to contact and ask if they knew John Mitchell, especially after she had known she was pregnant. The man should know he was to become a father. To no avail. No one she talked to claimed to know him. It was as if he vanished from the face of the earth.

Until now.

Quickly she read the article. A ranch was mentioned in Tumbleweed, Texas. She remembered his wild and outlandish stories of the family ranch. Most she'd taken with a grain of salt, but the basis had to be true, she'd thought. No wonder she had never found him in the city phone books, he lived in a town she'd never heard of—fifty miles west of Fort Worth.

The gist of the article centered on the magnificent grant he and his family provided. One million dollars.

Anger began to simmer. His disappearance had cheated Joey of knowing his father. And from the article, he had the means to have given Joey proper care from the beginning. She had been saving for more than four years for the operation that would enable Joey's eyes to track properly. Scraping together every dime she could manage, doing without so they could add to the surgery fund.

She only needed two thousand dollars more and her son would have surgery which would make eyes track like everyone else.

A man who could donate one million dollars to a charity, could certainly pony up a mere two thousand dollar for his own son's operation.

She reread the article. The money had been donated in memory of his wife and daughter.

So he'd gone back home and married some Texas girl. She'd long ago acknowledged the emotions she'd felt for John Mitchell Holden had been one-sided. No man, no matter how he professed to love her, would have stayed away and never contacted her. He knew where she lived. He could have called or written or come back to Fort Lauderdale if she'd meant anything to him.

The feelings she'd had for him had died long ago.

But Joey was his son. And by Jove, she was going to let the man know about the boy. Every child deserved a father. Maybe Joey's father could pay his fair share of the needed operation.

And if he gave her any grief, wouldn't the Dallas paper love to hear how the generous man and his family refused to help his own son!

Rising, Ginny strode into the café anxious for her shift to end. As soon as she was finished, she was calling John Mitchell Holden. Armed with the name of the town, she was sure she could find him with no trouble at all. Wouldn't he be surprised to hear a voice from the past?

CHAPTER ONE

GINNY peered through the rain at the ornate wrought-iron gate that marked the entrance to the Circle H Ranch. She sneezed again and blew her nose. Rubbing her aching chest, she tried to take a deep breath. It hurt to breathe.

This had been the trip from hell. If the blasted man had answered any of her letters, or returned a single phone call, she would not have had to drive from Florida to Texas. But he had ignored her as completely this past month as he had over the last five years.

Not that Ginny was going to let his behavior stop her. She'd taken a week's vacation from work, pushed her ancient car to the limit and here they were in Tumbleweed, Texas, turning onto the Holden Ranch.

The car had broken down in Biloxi. And again in that raging thunderstorm outside of Beaumont. Her cold had gotten worse by the day, made even more so after standing in the pouring rain while talking to the tow truck driver. Determined, she pushed on. She was not going to be ignored or blown off. If John Mitchell Holden thought refusing to respond to her demands would make her forget them, he didn't know her.

Of course, she thought as they inched up the drive in the downpour, he *hadn't* known her—not really. A brief two week fling was one thing. Romantic and exciting, but not of the real world.

More fool her for believing him when he told her he loved her. Hadn't her aunt warned her time after time? If she'd only listened. Yet if she had, she wouldn't have Joey, and she wouldn't trade him for anything. Wouldn't John Mitchell wish to learn he had a son?

"Are we there yet Mommy?" Joey asked from his car seat in the back.

"Almost, honey," she responded, hoping it was true. Truth to tell she hoped she could last long enough to challenge John Mitchell and get his agreement to help pay for the surgery before they had to leave to find a motel for the night. She wanted nothing more than to crawl into bed and pull the covers over her head and sleep until morning.

Florida was famous for summer afternoon thundershowers, but she was beginning to wonder if Texas had them beat. This was the third stormy day in a row.

"Will we see horses?" he asked.

"I don't know, they might be inside because of the rain." They could see plenty of cattle grazing in the fields flanking the road, but no horses.

"How about cows?" he persisted.

"Look out your window, there are more cows than you can count."

The huge herd covered several acres, many of the steers standing stoically, backs lined up to the wind, placidly enduring the rain as it poured down.

The driveway was like a county road, two lanes wide, paved and straight as an arrow. How far to the house? Cresting a slight rise, Ginny had her answer. Ahead rose a huge house, white, two stories tall with soaring columns supporting the roof that covered a wide veranda. It looked large enough to hold a multigenerational family. It reminded her of Tara—a bit splashy, but suitable for a family who could donate one million dollars to charity.

Beyond the house were the ranch buildings, two huge barns and an assortment of other buildings and sheds. She hadn't a clue about how ranches worked. What were all the structures for? A small brick building sat to the left of the house. It looked like an office to her, squat, with tall windows—looking like many insurances offices in Florida.

''Wow,'' Ginny thought, stunned at the size of the place. She slowed the car and stared. She had thought John Mitchell's bragging had been the wild tales of a college guy on the prowl out to impress. It looked as if he hadn't exaggerated one bit.

Suddenly doubt crept in.

Was she doing the right thing? Maybe she should have left Joey with her friend Maggie and come alone. Suddenly a horrifying thought sprang to mind. What if John Mitchell wanted visiting rights?

Or even custody?

According to the article, he'd lost his wife and child in a terrible automobile accident. Maybe he'd want his son near him. She felt a pang of sympathy for the man, even though she remained angry at his behavior toward her. How awful to lose a wife, but more especially a child. He wouldn't want Joey permanently, would he?

Ginny hesitated, wondering if she'd made the trip

for nothing. She'd taken precious funds from their savings for this trip, but she considered it well spent if she could get Joey's father to pay the balance of the expense. Doubts not withstanding, she couldn't turn back without seeing him, without trying to get him to pay a share, not when she was this close. And he deserved to meet his son. She hoped he'd like Joey, but be content to leave their current living arrangement intact.

"Why aren't we driving, Mommy? I see a house. The lights are on and it's only afternoon."

"I know, sweetie. It's because of the rain."

It was shortly after noon, yet it was so dark from the storm she needed her headlights. The glow through the windows in the house gave the illusion of welcome. Slowly she headed forward. She'd come all this way, she needed to see it through. For Joey's sake.

Stopping near the front door, Ginny turned off the engine and reached back to unfasten Joey's safety belt. "Climb over the seat and let's go," she said. Coughing for a moment, she waited while he scrambled over the seat back and stood beside her. She really felt awful. She hoped this encounter would go smoothly.

"We'll walk really fast so we don't get soaked, okay," she said. If she'd had an umbrella she would have tried to carry him and kept them both dry, but she hadn't thought to bring one. And she felt so tired and weak she didn't think she could carry him the short distance to the veranda. Maybe she should have gotten a room in Tumbleweed first, taken a nap and then come. Too late now.

She thrust open her door and hurried them to the front of the house.

"Whee," Joey said as he splashed in puddles between the car and the covered veranda.

Great, Ginny thought, as she tried to hurry him along. They'd both show up looking like drowned rats.

She rang the doorbell and shivered slightly in the breeze. Her shoulders and hair were damp from their mad dash. The wind cooled her quickly, blowing through her wet clothes as if she wore nothing.

The door opened. An older Mexican woman stood in the opening, her dark hair streaked with gray, bounded at the back of her head in a tidy bun. Her full skirted dress was covered by a large apron. "Can I help you?" she asked. She held a dish towel in one hand. Her expression was pleasant but curious.

"I'm looking for John Mitchell Holden," Ginny said.

Joey peeked around her to look at the woman, his eyes wide.

"Señor Holden is busy. Was he expecting you?"

"No, but we've come a long way. I just need a few minutes of his time." Ginny had come too far to be turned away. She was prepared to wait for however long it took.

The older woman studied Ginny for a moment, then looked at Joey, her expression softening into a smile.

"Step in out of the storm. I'll tell the señor you are here if you give me your name."

"Ginny Morgan." No sooner had she said it than she began coughing again. Her chest hurt so bad. And she felt flushed. They kept the house too warm, or was it the contrast to the coldness from the storm?

"Who is it Rosita?" a male voice called.

Ginny turned and watched as a stranger strode into the entryway. He frowned when he looked at her and then spotted Joey.

His hair was dark and cut short. His forbidding expression made him look even more intimidating than his size alone would have done. He was several inches over six feet, muscular and tanned. For a moment she remembered the skinny college kids who strutted so arrogantly on the beach during spring break. She couldn't imagine this man ever looking like that. But she suspected he could give them all lessons on sex appeal and how to capture a woman's attention.

Despite feeling terrible because of her cold, Ginny was intrigued.

The rugged jaw told Ginny he wasn't someone to be trifled with. His tanned skin attested to hours spent in the sun. His fit body didn't come from some gym. Was he a relative of John Mitchell's? Too young to be his father, was he an older brother? She guessed he was not too many years older than thirty.

A cough caught her. Her perusal cut short, she didn't have time to speculate. She was on a mission— as soon as she could catch her breath.

"I'm looking for John Mitchell Holden," Ginny said firmly.

"You've found him," the man said.

She blinked. The world seem to tilt and sway.

Joey peeped around her leg and looked up at the man.

"Are you my Daddy?" he asked.

It was the last thing Ginny heard before everything went black as she softly sank to the floor.

Mitch dashed forward barely catching her before her head hit the hardwood floor.

"Mommy?" The little boy clung to his mother's leg as she sagged in Mitch's arms. "Mommy, what's wrong?" His eyes wide with fear, the child clung to Ginny.

Mitch shifted and lifted her. "Your mom will be okay, son. Let me take her in the living room to lie down."

He carried her into the spacious room and placed her on the wide sofa. The little boy ran to her head and patted her shoulder. "Mommy?" Fear laced his tone.

"She'll be okay," Mitch said again, studying the unconscious woman, hoping she would come around soon. Color stained her cheeks, her breathing was raspy. She couldn't weigh more than a hundred pounds, which on her made her too thin.

"Should I call the doctor," Rosita asked poised in the doorway her face full of concern.

"Not yet. Let's see if she wakes up in a minute on her own," Mitch said, studying the unconscious woman. Just what he didn't need, a further complication to an already complicated day.

"I'll get a cool cloth," she said, heading for the back of the house.

This was not the best of times for unexpected visitors. Not when his long-term secretary had just informed him she was needed at home on a family emergency and would be leaving that afternoon. Her mother had fallen and broken her hip, there was no one else to see to the elderly woman but Helen. Still, the timing couldn't have been worse.

Not when he had a minor crisis building into a major one in Los Angeles.

Not when it was time to muster the herd and rotate cattle from the winter pasture to summer fields. He'd come home to the ranch for that event, which had already be delayed once this spring and was currently delayed because of the weather. If not for the muster, he'd still be in Dallas, or maybe even on the way to L.A.

He had a dozen irons in the fire, he did not need further complications.

"Why is Mommy asleep?" the boy asked. "She never takes naps."

"What's your name, son?" he asked. He'd never seen either of them before, but hadn't imagined the child's comment, *"Are you my daddy?"* Who were these people?

"I'm Joey," he said, "Is Mommy going to wake up soon?

"I expect so. Joey who? Where are you from?"

Joey wrinkled his brow as he looked up at Mitch.

He felt a hitch when he saw the uncertainty in the child's eyes. For a heartbeat they reminded him of Daisy's bright blue eyes. Except in this case one definitely turned inward. He didn't know much about it, but shouldn't the child have had some corrective work done by this age?

Rosita hurried into the room, carrying a cool, damp cloth. She placed it on Ginny's forehead and felt her cheeks with the back of her fingers. ''She had a fever, señor.''

''Who is she?''

''Her name is Ginny Morgan. She asked for you, said she came a long way to see you. Maybe we ought to call the doctor,'' she murmured.

The little boy looked up at him. ''Are you my Daddy?'' he asked again.

''No.'' Mitch knew that for a fact. Not only had he never seen the woman before in his life, the boy looked to be about four or five years old. And five years ago, he'd been a happily married man. Cheating on his wife had never once occurred to him, he'd loved Marlisse more than life.

The familiar ache gripped him. Would he ever get over losing her? Ever get used to the gaping hole in his heart that she and Daisy had once filled?

''Mommy said we were coming to meet my Daddy. Where is he?''

Mitch's instincts went on alert. She'd asked for him by name and told her son he was his father. What kind of scam was the woman trying to pull?

With her blond hair and gray eyes, and the boy's blue eyes, there was no way they could accuse him of being the father, not with his dark hair and eyes. DNA testing would cinch it if needed.

''Mommy,'' Joey said, shaking her. ''Wake up, Mommy.''

Mitch felt a tightening in his throat. The kid looked scared to death. He remembered Daisy when she had been five. All bright laughter and boundless energy. Nothing had scared her.

No child should be so scared.

He squatted down beside the youngster and took one small hand in his. Memories crowded in. He remembered holding Daisy's hand when they crossed a street, or went to a store. Echoes of her laughter sounded. He could still see her delight in so many everyday things.

This child looked nothing like his daughter, but just his being here reminded Mitch of all he'd lost.

"Where do you live, Joey?"

"Seventeen-thirty   Atlantic   Circle,   Fort Lauderdale," the boy said proudly. Obviously his mother made sure he knew his address.

"Florida?" Mitch murmured, wondering if Daisy had known her address at that age.

"We've been driving forever, and Mommy said we'd see my Daddy when we got here. We need money for my eyes. Once I have my operation, I can be just like all the other little boys, but until then, I'm special."

Rosita threw Mitch a look. "Shall I take the boy into the back so you can talk to the mother when she wakens?" she asked practically.

"I can't leave Mommy," Joey protested.

"Your Mommy's going to be fine," Mitch said, standing. "Let her rest for a few minutes. Rosita can give you a cookie and some milk. I bet you're hungry."

Joey seemed to consider the offer. "I am hungry. We didn't get lunch yet. Can I have lunch?" Joey asked.

"Sure thing. Rosita, would you?" When the housekeeper led the little boy away, he reached for the phone. It rang directly to the office.

"Yes, boss?" Helen answered, recognizing the inter-ranch line.

"Before you leave, call Jed Adams for me. I have a young woman who fainted in the entryway. She seems to have a fever and labored breathing. See if he thinks we need to bring her into emergency."

"Will do." Helen disconnected. Mitch almost smiled. Nothing fazed Helen. Not a stranger collapsing in the house, or anything else that happened around the ranch. She was as invaluable here as she was in the Dallas office. What the hell was he going to do with her gone for who knew how long?

And she didn't know how long she'd be gone. Helen had already called the local employment agency to send a temp, but Mitch knew it wouldn't be easy working with a stranger.

The woman began to stir. Good. If she came to, he could send her own her way, with a suggestion she stop off at the doctor's in town. One problem solved.

The phone rang just as those gray eyes opened again.

"Holden," Mitch responded when he picked up.

"Mitch? Heard you have someone who might need medical assistance," Jed Adams voice came across the line. He and Mitch had gone to high school together. Jed had then gone to study medicine while Mitch had specialized in business. Their paths didn't cross often these days, but the bond of friendship remained strong.

"I think she's coming out of it. Hold on," Mitch squatted again beside the sofa, his eyes almost on a level with hers.

"Are you feeling better?" he asked.

Slowly she blinked and stared at him. "What happened?" Her gaze darted around the room, confusion evident.

"Where's Joey?" A hint of panic sounded in her voice. She tried to sit up, but Mitch put his hand on her shoulder and pressed her back against the cushions.

"He's fine, in with Rosita having lunch. It's you we're concerned with. You fainted."

"Fainted! I never faint!" She rubbed her forehead. "I don't feel too well."

Mitch put the receiver back to his ear. "She's awake and lucid. I think the crisis has passed. I'll send her in to see you. Thanks for calling, Jed."

"No problem. Let me know if you need anything."

Mitch hung up the phone and rose to his full height. At over six feet, she had a long way to look up. The confusion hadn't left her expression.

"You are not John Mitchell Holden," she said quietly.

"Was the last time I looked. But obviously not the one you were expecting. Never knew there were two of us."

She closed her eyes, tears seeping from between the lids.

"Can I get you something?" Mitch asked, wondering who Ginny Morgan was, and why she was looking for him—or rather some man who had the same name.

She shook her head. "I'll be out of your way in a minute. Sorry for the misunderstanding. I thought—I saw an article in the Dallas paper that reported your donation to the Children's Last Wish Foundation. I

thought I had found the man I've been looking for
for years. I mean, I thought you were John Mitchell.
My John Mitchell Holden. Actually not mine, exactly.
But I've been looking for him for five years. I thought
I'd finally located him.''

"You came a long way based on a newspaper article. Your son said you live in Florida.''

"I tried writing, calling, but you would never respond. I was desperate.''

"Because?''

Mitch sat on the chair flanking the sofa. Before
Ginny could say another word, his aunt Emaline
swirled into the room, her lacy dress more suitable
for a garden party than the ranch house. But he was
used to it. Fancy feminine dresses were her standard
wardrobe. He sighed. Another complication he did
not need!

"Oh, nephew, I'm so pleased you knew to call on
me in case of an emergency. I'm happy to help in
any way I can. Is this the poor dear. Oh, she does
look ill.''

Ginny stared at the elderly woman, delicate in
statue with soft white hair curled around her face. Her
dress reminded her of Southern parties and gentile
living. Feminine and flighty, Ginny summed up in one
thought. And a bit out of place in the room which
had a strong southwest decor.

She glanced at the rugged man who looked pained
for a split second at the arrival of the older woman.
He quickly schooled his features.

Could they really be in the same family? She'd
called him nephew, but he looked too large, too masculine to be connected to this ethereal woman.

"How do you feel, dear?" She fluttered over and patted Ginny's cheeks. "Oh, you are burning up. Mitch," she looked at her nephew, "she's burning up. We need to give her something for the fever. Aspirin. I think aspirin would be fine. And fluids. Plenty of fluids. Clear like apple juice or water."

When Ginny began coughing, Emaline raised her handkerchief to her cover her nose and mouth, still fluttering around.

"Oh dear, that cough is terrible. Mitch, we must do something about that as well. Bed rest will help. Should she have the lilac room or the rose? Lilac I think, it's so soothing, and the rose will confuse the issue about her fever, don't you think? She's flushed enough without pink from the walls."

"What?" Mitch looked at his aunt. What issue?

"The rose room will make her skin look rosy, how will we tell if the fever is gone?"

"If she were staying, we could use a thermometer," he said, standing. "But the issue won't arise because she's not staying."

"Mitch, you can't send an ill woman out into a storm like this. I won't hear of it."

"Aunt Emaline, she is a total stranger. I don't know anything about her. She came here from Florida, I'm sure she can make it as far as town where she can get a motel room."

"I'll be on my way. I'm sorry for the problem I caused." Ginny tried to stand, her knees feeling like soggy spaghetti noodles. She fell back to the sofa with a soft plop.

"See?" Emaline said triumphantly. "She can't possibly travel. If you don't wish to put her up, I will.

It would be crowded in the cottage, of course, but I won't shirk my duty to the less fortunate by sending a sick person out on a day like this!''

Mitch suppressed the urge to roll his eyes at the familiar dramatic flare his aunt was famous for. He nodded once. He would speak to Rosita for calling his aunt. If she hadn't arrived, he could have sent the stranger and her child on her way with no compunction. Now he'd be stuck with her for at least a day. Hopefully by tomorrow she'd be better and could head back to Florida.

''Then I'll leave her in you capable hands, Aunt Emaline.''

''I'll take care of everything Mitch. You go on back to work. Ask Rosita to help me, will you?'

''She's busy right now with the little boy.''

Emaline's eyes grew wide as saucers. ''Little boy? Why didn't you say so? Oh, it's been too long since this house has heard the ring of childish laughter. Where is he?''

''In the kitchen.'' Yes it had been too long since he'd heard childish laughter. It would forever be too long.

She almost ran from the room in her quest to see the child.

Mitch sighed and looked at the woman now sitting on the sofa, holding a hand against her chest, rubbing absently. The coughing had stopped. The bright spots of color in her cheeks attested to the fever.

She watched him with a wary expression. Except for the two spots of red staining each cheek with brilliant color, she was pale and wan.

"I'll leave in a few minutes. I can't stay here," she said.

"Emaline has the right to invite whomever she wishes to stay. I can show you a bedroom large enough for you and your son. Or I can fix him up another room, so he doesn't get what you have."

"If he were going to get it, four days in a car would have exposed him," she said.

"It took you four days to get here from Fort Lauderdale?"

She nodded. "We had car trouble." Ginny watched him carefully, studying his features. He looked nothing like the college guy she'd fallen for. He was the wrong age, the wrong size, the wrong coloring and definitely not the kind of man she'd want to tangle with.

"You've come a long way on the basis of a newspaper article." He waited for something more, the suggestion of help she needed, maybe money for the return journey? Was she hoping for the sympathy play? Donations of that magnitude reported in the paper had already resulted in dozens of requests from other organizations. Helen was fielding them all, but Ginny Morgan was the first individual to respond in person—that he knew of. Of course Helen would be screening those as well.

"I thought it was fate. That I found John Mitchell Holden just when I most needed him. He said he was from Texas, his family had a ranch. He told me stories about the place, but maybe it was all made up."

"When was this?"

"Five years ago. At spring break in Fort Lauderdale."

"Wild spring break, fun parties and no responsibilities. You met him there?"

Ginny stiffened at the derision of his tone. What happened in her past was none of his business!

Ginny rubbed her forehead again, her eyes closing. She wished she could find a bed and sleep for twelve hours.

"Life goes on. I'll get out of your way, Mr. Holden. Sorry to have bothered you."

"Stay the night as Aunt Emaline suggested. The storm isn't easing and it'll be treacherous driving in it. If you aren't familiar with our roads, navigating them in a storm is to be avoided at all costs. Besides, the Circle H is known for its hospitality."

At least it had been with Marlisse had been its mistress. She loved having friends over, entertaining, cooking for a crowd, and showing off the ranch. No one had stayed the night since she'd been gone. Rosita would have to make the beds, air out the rooms as best she could with this storm.

He looked out the window. The wind had the trees bent under its force. The rain was coming down in sheets. The last thing he wanted was some stranger and her appealing little boy in his house overnight. But his aunt was right. He wouldn't send anyone out in this—especially a sick woman and a child.

"Have you ever heard of another Holden family in ranching?" Ginny asked hopefully.

"As far as I know, there are no other Holdens who own ranches in Texas. I've been a member of the Cattleman's Association for years, I'm sure I'd have heard if there were others in Texas."

"He was blond, with bright blue eyes. Joey got his

eyes," she murmured. "Maybe the whole thing was a line. For all I know he's a druggist in New Jersey."

Slowly she toppled over to her side. "Though he did have a Texas drawl," she murmured as she succumbed to sleep.

"Well, hell," Mitch thought as he watched her fall asleep. Once Rosita had the room ready, Mitch would rouse his uninvited guest, or carry her, let her sleep the night. If she wasn't better by morning, he'd call Jed again and have his friend come out.

But what was he going to do with the boy? He had buried his wife and daughter. He'd never planned to be around children again. He avoided family gatherings, had made it clear to his sister and cousins he wasn't in the mood for company.

Emaline wanted them to stay. She could entertain the child. She'd have her work cut out trying to amuse a young boy. But she was on her own. He was not going to become involved.

Maybe Jack Parlance's wife could take charge of Joey, if he proved too much for Emaline. The foreman's wife had raised three boys of her own, all out working on their own, now. She'd know what to do with one little boy.

And she'd relish the opportunity, while to him it would cause only anguish.

He turned and strode from the room, angry at fate for interrupting his routine. He didn't need Helen going off. Didn't need Ginny Morgan or her cute little boy invading his life. And he sure as hell didn't need to know someone had been impersonating him five years ago!

CHAPTER TWO

GINNY awoke slowly and stretched beneath the covers. For the first time in ages her headache was finally gone. She opened her eyes slowly, then sat up. A strange bed in a strange room. Where was she? This wasn't her bedroom, nor one of the anonymous motel rooms they'd stayed in on their way to Texas.

The sun shone from a clear sky. Through the tall windows dressed in crisp white Priscilla curtains, she could see the rolling Texas hills, dotted with cattle.

Memory returned. She was at the Circle H Ranch. Vaguely she remembered talking with John Mitchell Holden—only not her John Mitchell Holden, some man they called Mitch who looked nothing like the carefree college student whom she'd once loved.

She remembered the out-of-place Emaline and Joey talking about horses and a stranger taking her temperature. Hadn't there a also an injection? It was all blurred. Had it been a dream?

Gingerly she pushed back the light covers and rose, quickly grasping the headboard. She felt weak and shaky. How sick was she? Her chest no longer hurt, her cough seemed gone.

The door opened and Rosita peeked in. "Ah, you are awake. And getting up? That is good. I will tell Señorita Emaline and then bring breakfast." Before Ginny could respond, she'd shut the door.

Ginny sat on the edge of the bed and looked

around. Where was Joey? How long had they been here? She seemed to remember various people popping in and out, but was that real or some dream? She saw her suitcase on a stand near the door. Rising again, she crossed over and found a clean set of clothes. Spying the en suite bathroom, she headed for it to shower and dress. She couldn't believe she had stayed in a stranger's home.

Taking a deep breath, she felt relief, her chest no longer hurt. Thank goodness for that. She'd dress, find Joey and be on their way. The trip had been for nothing. She still had not found the man she was searching for. The disappointment threatened to overwhelm her. Not only would they not be getting the funds needed for the operation, she had used several hundred dollars from the operation savings for this futile trip.

By the time she was finished dressing, Ginny wanted to crawl back into bed and sleep another twenty-four hours. But Rosita had set up a lovely breakfast at the small round table by the tall windows. A light omelet was centered on the plate, fresh fruit beside it. A tall glass of orange juice and a cup of fragrant coffee completed the meal. She didn't know where to begin.

Where was Joey? She sipped the orange juice and wondered if she should take the time to eat before seeking her son. She'd relinquished his care to Rosita yesterday, certainly a few more minutes might not hurt. And she was famished!

She ate slowly, savoring each delicious bite. Some Mexican kind of omelet, she thought, enjoying the blend of unknown spices and peppers. She'd ask for the recipe before she left.

They needed to get moving. Her week's vacation would be over before they returned home at the rate they were going. Though she hoped to make better time returning. Fingers crossed the car didn't break down again.

She could ill afford to keep it repaired. Every dollar she expended on the trip meant that much taken from their operation account. She was farther behind than when they'd started. She'd been so sure she'd find Joey's father. Now what was she going to do?

A soft knock on the door presaged Emaline's arrival. Today she wore a soft rose dress, lace at the neck and on the cuffs of the sheer, long sleeves. Ballet slippers completed the ensemble and she seemed to float along as she crossed the room to the table.

"Oh, you are awake at last. I'm so glad. How are you feeling? We've been so worried about you. But Jed said you would be fine, just needed lots of rest and nourishment. And he did give you a shot since you couldn't take a pill with all your coughing. But the broth Rosita kept fixing didn't seem like enough food and you wouldn't ever drink it all. I think a nice poached egg would have been divine, but Mitch said the broth would have to do."

Emaline took the chair opposite and beamed at Ginny.

"And Joey is such a treasure. He much brings so much delight. It's been too long since this house had a child it in. Of course we all miss Daisy dreadfully, but she's been gone two years. And I think a big house deserves lots of children running through it, don't you? We had seven in our family. Mama said that was six too many sometimes, but she loved us all dearly. And we all loved her and Papa dearly. My younger sister married Bradley Holden. They're Mitch's parents. The ranch belongs to Bradley of course, though Mitch runs it now that his parents are traveling. It's been in their family for generations. I have a small cottage in the back. Isn't Rosita's omelet delicious? I do like a spicy omelet. But of course I cook for myself most of the time, only coming over to join Mitch when he's here. Or even when he travels if Rosita has made something special.''

Ginny tried to follow the conversation, feeling her head spin at the rapid pace of Emaline's change of topics. When the woman paused to take a breath, Ginny interrupted.

''Where's Joey?''

''He's out with the horses. The child is crazy for them. If he were staying, I'd bet he'd be riding before you knew it. Daisy rode when she was only three. Of course Mitch got her a safe pony. He gave it away after her death. But he would never take a chance with a child, so if you were to stay, I'm sure he'd get another quiet pony for Joey. Not that he's had much to do with the child. He has closed his heart to most thing, living for work alone. He's increased the family coffers substantially, so none of us are complaining, but it would be nice to see him settled again. And not so driven.''

Ginny assumed the Daisy she spoke of was the daughter who had died. Hearing about her made her even more real. She couldn't even imagine the full anguish of losing a child. It had to be the greatest heartache there was.

''There,'' Emaline said beaming as Ginny ate the

last bite of omelet. "It was delicious, wasn't it? I'm so glad to see you eating at last."

Ginny looked at her. "At last?"

"Four days with nothing but broth makes a person very weak, don't you think?" Emaline tilted her head as she looked at Ginny.

"*Four days?* I've been here four days?" Ginny was horrified. She couldn't have imposed on total strangers for four whole days!

Mitch couldn't believe one snide comment would cause tears, histrionics and a slammed door. The temp had left in a flurry, leaving him alone in the front office trying to make some sense of Helen's filing process. He pulled out another folder, glanced inside and replaced it. Maybe he should pull in one of the men off the ranch, they at least wouldn't take offense at the slightest thing.

His secretary had not called to give him an estimated return date. He was growing impatient with the temps the sole agency in town was sending. Two in three days. Couldn't they find the right person—someone competent enough to do routine office tasks? Or if not that, at least someone who wouldn't take off at the first hint of complaint?

A small sound alerted him he was no longer alone. Mitch glanced up and saw Joey Morgan standing in the doorway.

"Kids aren't allowed in the office," Mitch said. He had a conference call in ten minutes and hoped he could find the Montgomery folder before then.

"The lady was saying bad words," Joey said, walking in.

"I heard," Mitch said. Maybe he shouldn't have asked if she knew the alphabet in such a sarcastic manner. But dammit, that folder was important and she hadn't been able to find it. Not that he was having much better luck. Maybe his remark had been made in haste.

"Mommy never says bad words. She says we can be more creative and show we're smarter than people who copy other people to say bad words," he said solemnly.

Mitch looked at Joey. Hadn't he told the boy no kids allowed in the office?

"Is Mommy going to get better today?" Joey asked coming closer.

"I don't know. Probably." Ah, the folder he'd wanted. Mitch pulled it free, and returned to his desk. He opened it, then looked at Joey who had moved to press against his side, peering in curiosity at the things on the wide surface of his desk.

"Look, kid, I have work to do. Children aren't allowed in the office."

"Mr. Parlance said since my mommy is sick, I have to ask you if I can ride. I really want to be a cowboy. Can I ride one of your horses?"

Mitch shook his head. "No."

Joey didn't pester him like Daisy would have at the refusal. He merely hitched his shoulders a little and looked disappointed.

Mitch studied him covertly. The kid was well behaved and not a pest. Jack said he ate up every word any of the cowboys said, and hung for hours on the corral fence talking to the horses and petting any that ambled his way.

Damn shame about his eyes. What was his mother going to do about that? It wasn't fair to the kid to have that kind of problem and not have the adults in his life take care of it.

Just then Ginny Morgan rushed into the office.

"Mr. Holden, I had no idea I'd been here this long!" she said.

"Mommy!" Joey brightened instantly and ran to her.

The phone rang.

"Joey." She swung him up into her arms hugging him closely.

"Are you all better?" he asked.

"Holden," Mitch said into the phone, watching Ginny and his son. The images blurred and he saw Marlisse swing up their daughter. She had adored Daisy. God, he'd loved them both so much. Missed them every day.

He turned away, forcing his gaze to move to the folder, ignoring the scene unfolding near the office door. He had work to do and the sooner he became involved, the sooner the piercing pain would fade.

"Mitch says I can't ride. Can you get me a horse?" Joey asked his mother.

Conscious of her reluctant host on the phone, she stepped into the outer office. "Shh, he's busy. No, we can't get a horse. We need to get back home. Tom's going to be mad as it is. I'm already late returning to work and haven't even let him know we're still in Texas."

"I like it here."

"Home is best," Ginny said, relishing the feel of her little boy. He struggled to get down. She never got to hold him as long as she wanted anymore. He was growing up too fast.

Glancing around, Ginny was amazed as the high-tech feel to the office. Emaline's rambles had included information about Mitch, and every other person in a twenty-five mile radius, she suspected.

But it was the newly acquired knowledge that Mitch ran the family holdings that had fascinated her. She'd thought he was a rancher, and while Emaline assured her he lived for part of the year on the ranch, he also had penthouse apartments in Los Angeles, New York and Dallas. According to Emaline, it was nothing unusual for Mitch and his personal assistant to take off on short notice for one or the other city when business demanded.

"Want to come see the horses, Mommy?" Joey asked, struggling to be let down.

She put him on his feet, and brushed his cheek. Leaning against the desk, she shook her head. "Not just yet. I want to talk to Mr. Holden." She glanced through the opened door and wondered how long he'd be on the phone. She felt embarrassed to have stayed so long in his house. While she still felt a little shaky, she knew she'd infringed on his hospitality long enough. After thanking him, she'd pack Joey's things and head back for Florida. Her suitcase was all ready to go.

"Can I go see the horses?" Joey asked. "Mr. Parlance said it's okay as long as I stay out of the corral. I just climb up the fence, I never go inside the corral."

"Is that what you've been doing while I was sick?" Ginny asked, brushing back his hair. How could she have been unaware of the passage of four days!

He nodded, his eyes shining.

"Okay, then, if it's all right with those in charge. But we aren't staying long. We have to get back home. As soon as I speak with Mr. Holden, we'll be on our way."

His face fell. "Oh, do we have to? I love it here. They've got horses and cows and dogs and even a cat in the barn, but I can't pat her because she doesn't much cotton to people."

Ginny almost laughed at Joey's phrasing. Who had he been talking to?

"Then run along and say your goodbyes."

Ginny watched Joey scamper away. Hearing Mitch's voice in the background, she suspected his call would last a few minutes. Tired, she moved to sit in the chair behind the desk. She still felt weak, wobbly. And mortified she'd been four days imposing on these kind people. How could she have been so sick?

According to Emaline the doctor had said it was borderline pneumonia. They must think her crazy to show up at their front door so ill. But she'd truly thought it just a cold.

She would offer to pay Mitch for their expenses. It would take even more from the operation fund, but that couldn't be helped. She would not be beholden to anyone. Her aunt Edith had harped on that all the years Ginny had lived with her.

Closing her eyes, she rested her head on the back of the chair. As soon as she'd finished with Mitch Holden, she'd find a motel in Tumbleweed and stay another day to rest up. By tomorrow she'd be ready to head for home.

She had better call Tom and make sure he knew she hadn't disappeared off the face of the earth. And a quick call to her friend Maggie, too. She'd be anxious to know the outcome of the trip.

Thinking of all she had to do, Ginny slowly drifted off to sleep.

Mitch hung up the phone, satisfied with the conversation. If Jim followed up as he'd promised, Mitch wouldn't have to take a trip to L.A. anytime soon.

Tossing the folder to the corner of the desk, he started to reach for the phone to call the temp agency. Tumbleweed wasn't large enough to support more than one agency, and their selection of potential employees was slim. Too bad. They'd just have to find someone else. The two they'd sent had not worked out.

He heard a chair squeak. Curious, he rose and crossed to the outer office. Ginny Morgan was asleep on Helen's chair. She was listing slightly to the left, and if she continued her slow slide, she'd fall over.

He reached out and shook her shoulder lightly. When she opened her eyes and looked up at him in sleepy confusion, he felt an odd unfurling deep within. She looked young, innocent and unaware of where she was. Her hair was a soft cloud of gold around her face, soft and silky. Her eyes shimmered in silvery lights.

For a moment Mitch yearned to touch that hair, to sift it through his fingers and feel its silken weight, let it flow around his hand like gossamer. To stare into the silvery pools of her eyes and forget all of yesterday's heartaches.

He frowned and jerked his hand away. What was he thinking? She was a troublesome visitor, nothing more. And he wanted nothing to do with any woman. He'd loved his wife. He'd been devastated by her death. He would not become involved again, even superficially. Death was too final, parting too painful.

"I'm sorry," she said, standing abruptly. "I fell asleep again. You must think I'm crazy. Usually I have tons of energy."

"You've been pretty sick. Should you even be up today?" he asked, studying her closely.

"I'm fine. Actually, we'll be leaving soon. I wanted to thank you for all your help. I'm, um, I wanted to reimburse you for any—"

He shook his head and stepped away before her light fragrance muddled his brain.

"No need. I hope you have a good journey home."

She smiled uncertainly. "Thank you. If you ever hear of another John Mitchell Holden, would you let me know? I'll leave my address and phone number."

He looked at her for a long moment. What were the chances of there really being another John Mitchell Holden? Had she come to attempt a scam? If so, why hadn't she followed through? Nothing had been said, nothing even hinted. If she was trying to run a con, she sure had a long way to go. Joey had mentioned getting money for his eyes, but Ginny Morgan had never raised the subject.

Maybe she was just what she said she was, a young mother searching for her child's father.

"If I ever hear of another man with my name, I'll let you know."

Ginny held out her hand. "Thank you again, Mr. Holden. I appreciate all your hospitality."

He shook her hand, surprised at the sensation he experienced when he touched her. Her hand was cool, firm in his. She didn't hold on, never tried to flirt, but the jolt of awareness was real.

"Tell me why you came here, Ginny Morgan," he said on a sudden impulse. "Joey said something about an operation for his eyes."

She nodded, raising her chin slightly. "I know you've seen how they are crossed. The insurance I have doesn't cover the cost for the operation, so I have been saving almost since he was born to pay for it." She shrugged. "When I saw the article in the newspaper about your family donating money to the Last Wish Foundation, I thought I'd found Joey's father. I thought—"

He waited a moment when she went silent.

"Thought you'd hit him up for it," he finished for her.

She flushed slightly. Mitch stared. He couldn't remember the last time he'd seen a woman blush. It didn't go with the image he'd formed, of a swinging single woman partying at the beach who had gotten caught with a baby.

"I'm only a couple of thousand short, I thought if he, you…I mean, I thought it was Joey's father who donated so much. And if he had that much to donate, then he could surely spare two thousand dollars for his own son." She ended all in a rush. "Joey's really a great little boy. And I hate for him to start school with the problem.''

Mitch rubbed the back of his neck. The few times he'd seen Joey, the kid had been upbeat and enthusiastic. He'd worried about his mother, then scampered off and been captivated by the horses. Jack reported he was no trouble, and was in fact eating up everything he learned.

Mitch could understand Ginny's determination. If Daisy had needed anything, he would have moved heaven and earth to get it for her. He turned and went to the door, looking out over the spread. He hadn't been able to do anything for his daughter. By the time he'd heard of the drunken driver crashing into his wife's car, both Marlisse and Daisy had been dead several hours.

But maybe he could help another child.

He turned and glanced around the room.

''Do you know anything about office work?'' he asked.

CHAPTER THREE

"NOT much," Ginny said, surprised at the question. Waiting tables was nothing like working in an office.

"Can you type, answer the phones?" he persisted.

She thought about the hours she's spent on the Internet searching for Joey's father while Joey enjoyed storybook time in the library. About the endless letters she'd typed on the library computers and sent out—always searching.

"I can type, but not fast. And anyone can answer a phone."

"I need secretarial help," he said. "Helen, my personal assistant, had to leave on a family emergency a few days ago. I've had two incompetent women in since then, and the office is in more chaos than if I hadn't had anyone."

"I have a job waiting for me in Fort Lauderdale," Ginny said.

"I'll make you a deal. I'll make up the difference for Joey's surgery and he can have the operation in Dallas. In exchange, you work for me until Helen returns." That would solve the problem of a temp leaving in a huff.

Ginny stared at the man. He would pay for the surgery for a total stranger? What was the catch?

"How long is Helen going to be gone?"

"I have no idea, a couple of weeks, a couple of months. She's supposed to let me know when she has a better handle on things at her end. Do we have a deal?''

Ginny bit her lip, hope flooding. Did he mean it? He'd pay the balance for Joey's surgery if she worked in his office until Helen returned? Could she get Tom to hold her job until she got back to Florida?

Did she even care about that particular job if she got Joey's surgery taken care of? Good waitresses weren't as plentiful as people thought. She'd be able to get another job if Tom wouldn't take her back.

To have Joey get his eyes fixed immediately—long before he started school—she became almost giddy with the thought.

"Just office work?" she clarified. He wasn't expecting anything else was he? Not that she was some femme fatale, but his offer seemed too generous for mere secretarial work—especially for someone who had no office experience.

His P.A. could return before the surgery was even scheduled. Then what?

"I have a housekeeper, I don't need another one. And Emaline doubles as hostess when I have a need for one for business events. I only need help with office work," Mitch replied.

"I won't be fast or as efficient as a trained secretary," she warned. Was she an idiot? She should snap up his offer in a heartbeat, not feel slightly disappointed he had no designs outside the office.

The offer seemed too good to be true. There had to be a hidden string attached somewhere. But Ginny almost didn't care. The fact Joey would have his operation was all that mattered to her.

"I have several thousand dollars saved up. I'll have

my bank transfer it out here,'' she said. ''I don't need the entire operation paid for, just the difference from what I have saved.''

''I said I'd take care of the bill. You keep your money,'' Mitch said. ''We can settle all that after the operation. Are you up to starting now?''

''I can't believe you'd offer to do this for me. For Joey.''

Mitch narrowed his gaze as he looked at her. After a long moment, he said, ''I'm doing it for Daisy.''

The phone rang.

Ginny looked at it, then him. ''I start now?''

He hesitated, studying her pale features. ''Work until lunch, then rest up this afternoon. Time enough tomorrow to put in a full day.'' He nodded toward the phone, ''Answer it—Holden Enterprises.''

She picked up the phone, her voice rich and firm as she identified the business. She had seen enough television to know how topnotch secretaries acted. Too bad her faded jeans and loose top weren't sophisticated apparel, it ruined any competent image she could hope to give.

She covered the receiver.

''A Mr. Baker from a bank.''

''I'll take it in my office.''

Ginny held the receiver to her ear until she heard Mitch pick up, then hung up her phone. The vast array of buttons and numbers on the console phone had her confused. Of course a business office would have several phone lines. Was there an instruction booklet somewhere to give her a clue how to use the thing?

She sat back down, feeling breathless and excited. Mitch Holden was going to see to Joey's operation.

Her son would be completely normal within weeks. It felt as if a huge weight lifted from her shoulders at the generosity of one man.

But why was he doing this? Surely he could hire a secretary with no trouble. Why pay what would be the equivalent of an exorbitant fee for the length of time she'd be working?

And where was she going to live in the meantime? Who would take care of Joey? He couldn't just run wild around the ranch. She had to call Tom. She needed to call Maggie, her best friend, to tell her where she was, all that had happened. Maybe listen to a word of warning.

Ginny knew Daisy had been Mitch's daughter. Emaline had regaled her with enough stories about the little girl that Ginny felt she'd almost known her. Suddenly she frowned. She'd have to do the best job she could. She hoped his helping Joey would ease some of the pain from his daughter's loss.

Since Mitch seemed to spend most of his time on the phone, Ginny had gone through every drawer and file in Helen's desk by lunchtime—feeling as if she were trespassing. But Ginny wanted to do the best she could, learn as much as she could about how the office operated. Even so, she'd never be able to repay Mitch Holden for the gift he was giving.

She flipped through the Rolodex, noting names, wishing Helen had provided background on each person. Especially the cards that just had first names, like Hank or Sara.

Ginny had excellent recall. She often took the orders from a large group without aid of a notepad. If

Mitch asked her to call someone, she knew she'd remember if their name had been on the cards.

She didn't find a booklet to show her how to use the phone. Trial and error would have to suffice, she thought fatalistically when she disconnected a caller.

If Mitch Holden wanted her to know how to run the phone, he would have to show her, or let her learn as she went.

A separate phone, a single line, rang. Ginny lifted it.

"Holden Enterprises," she said brightly.

"Hi Mommy. Rosita said I could call you to see if you are coming to lunch. She made tacos and salad and other stuff!"

Ginny glanced at the clock, it was almost one. "Yes, I could go for some lunch. I'll be right there." The morning hours had flown by.

Mitch was on the phone—again. It hadn't stopped ringing since that first call. She'd found the message pads and carefully took names and numbers. Getting jumbled up on a couple of the messages, she figured he would know what the call was about.

Did she just leave for lunch? Should she let him know she was leaving?

She went to the door to his office, the stack of phone messages in hand. He looked up and covered the receiver with his hand.

"Do you need something?" he asked.

"Joey called and said Rosita had prepared lunch."

"Bring me back a plate." With that, he resumed his phone conversation.

She placed the stack of notes on his desk and took off.

Ginny savored the warm sunshine as she crossed from the office to the main house. The sky was cloudless. The air was scented with dried grass and the hint of cattle and horses. What a difference from the downpour when they had arrived.

She could hardly believe all that has transpired since that afternoon. First, Mitch had not been the man she was looking for. Then she'd fainted away like some Victorian wimp which made her feel totally a flake.

Being sick was not deliberate, but she still couldn't believe the hospitality of the Holdens to put her up for four days. And instead of demanding compensation, Mitch was going to pay for Joey's surgery! It all seemed like a dream. Would she awaken soon and find she was late for work?

Walking up the steps into the house, Ginny felt exhausted. Not that she'd admit that to anyone. She didn't want Mitch to think she wasn't up to the job and withdraw his offer. She hoped the midday meal would perk her up—maybe even enough to finish the day in the office.

Or it might be better to take Mitch up on his offer to take the afternoon off. She had to make plans for their stay in Texas. Hopefully Emaline would suggest a reasonably priced apartment complex. If she didn't return to work today, she could drive into Tumbleweed and find accommodation.

And a day care center for Joey.

There were tons of things to do, but none of them seemed insurmountable. After all, her darling little boy would soon have his eyes fixed.

Emaline and Joey were already seated at the large dining room table when Ginny joined them.

"Mitch not coming?" Emaline asked peering behind Ginny.

"He's on the phone, asked if I'd bring a plate. Should I take it first?"

"No, dear. Sit down and eat. You look pale. Maybe you should take a long nap this afternoon. You just got this morning up for the first time in four days. My mother always said a woman needed to look after herself because the menfolks surely wouldn't."

"Tacos, Mommy," Joey said, holding up a crisp corn tortilla filled with meat, lettuce and cheese.

"It looks delicious, sweetie." Ginny sat where Emaline indicated and soon had her own plate filled with a delicious taco salad. Rosita had made the traditional tacos for Joey. Ginny was surprised and touched at the extra effort the housekeeper had gone to for her son.

"Come with me to see the horses after lunch," Joey said.

"Your mother needs to rest," Emaline said emphatically.

"Oh, I can't. Mitch hired me to work in the office until his secretary gets back. I don't have time for a nap. There's so much to do."

"Nonsense. You're exhausted, I can tell. A quick nap is important. I'll tell the man myself."

Visions of being fired before the day ended flashed through Ginny's mind.

"I'm fine. Lunch will give me plenty of energy. And I'm grateful for the job. I don't want to jeopardize it."

"Aunt Emaline said she would go with me to the horses, can't you, too?" Joey said.

"Joey! She's not your aunt."

"I asked the child to call me aunt. It's little enough. I so love children. I loved being around while Mitch and his sister and cousins were little. Daisy was such a darling precious child."

"It must be so hard to lose a child," Ginny murmured.

"It is, even one not my own. She's been dead these two years now. She was eight when that damned drunken driver broadsided their car. She and Marlisse never had a chance, the police said." Emaline shook her head. "I didn't think Mitch would survive for a while. When he heard, he went crazy. Then he just closed himself off from everything."

Ginny's gaze moved to Joey, her own precious child. What would she do if something happened to him? How would she survive? If closing himself off worked for Mitch, more power to him. She though she'd probably die herself of a broken heart.

"Daisy was almost as horse crazy as Joey. She loved to ride. She had the sweetest pony. A lot of ponies aren't sweet, don't you know. But this one was. And she followed her dad around whenever he was home. Marlisse could only have the one child and they both doted on her."

"Mitch offered to pay the balance for Joey's operation," Ginny said, "saying it was for Daisy."

Emaline looked surprised. "Did he? How unexpected." She reached for more iced tea. "He always had a soft spot for kids. But since Daisy died, he's made it clear he doesn't want his niece or nephew visiting for long, or any of his cousins' children. I think their presence reminds him too strongly of Daisy's death.'' Emaline began to regale them with stories of the younger generation, and the antics they got into on the ranch.

"I'll need to find a place to stay, maybe you can give me some suggestions of where to look in Tumbleweed,'' Ginny said a little later when they were almost finished lunch.

"I wouldn't hear of it. You and Joey need to stay right here. I can watch him myself while you work. And Rosita loves children. She has seven herself and four grandchildren already. Besides, staying here will save time driving back and forth. If Joey is having an operation, he'll need care while he recovers, so where better than right here?'' Emaline beamed at Ginny, then winked at Joey.

Her rose colored dress was the perfect foil for her snowy white hair and pink cheeks. Ginny could feel the honesty in the woman's tone and actions. Emaline genuinely liked people and sincerely wanted to help. Ginny had the feeling Emaline would have done well as a hostess for some rich plantation owner in the olden days. She loved flowery, feminine clothes, had a graciousness about her that was endearing. And she loved children. What better person to watch her son when Ginny was unable to.

Except, Ginny couldn't let her.

What would Mitch say when he heard of his aunt's invitation? The job had not come with an offer of room and board. Ginny needed to be independent. And she could not infringe any longer on these people's hospitality.

She finished lunch quickly, promising to go see the horses with Joey once she had a chance. Taking a hot plate from Rosita, she hurried back to the office. Lunch had given her renewed energy. She still felt tired, but not too tired to slack off.

Mitch was standing by the fax machine when she entered, watching as page after page rolled out.

Ginny studied him for a moment before he realized she'd returned. The lines around his mouth could be contributed to sadness, she thought. Was the solemn way he viewed life a direct result of the blows life had dealt?

How sad he pushed other family members away. They might be able to help him remember the good times and get past the immediate pain of loss. Emaline had said it had been two years—not that there was a time limit on grieving. But he needed to move on and find happiness where he could. Ginny knew this from the death of her own parents, and more recently Aunt Edith. She had only Joey. How she would have welcomed family rallying around when her elderly aunt had died.

Mitch looked up and caught her gaze, then saw the plate. "Thanks. I'm hungry."

"Rosita piled it high, saying you needed to eat it all."

"If I ate all Rosita gave me, I'd need to bunk in the barn, none of the beds in the house would hold me."

Ginny grinned. Maybe he wasn't such a somber man after all.

"I can watch the papers for you if you want to eat. Will the machine jam?"

"No, I'm just waiting for the full report so I can read it."

"Go eat, I'll bring it in when it's all here," she said holding out the plate.

Mitch took it and went into his office. He was hungry enough to eat everything Rosita had sent. As he ate, he looked into the outer office. By angling his chair just so, he could see Ginny standing by the fax machine. She was faithfully watching each sheet as it came out, taking it and stacking it with the rest. Her jeans were loose on her. Had she lost weight because of being ill, or was she naturally thin? A few weeks of Rosita's food and she'd plump up a bit.

He looked away, scowling. He didn't care if she did or did not fill out. She was merely a stranger who was going to help him out until Helen came back. A stranger with silky blond hair and sparkling silvery eyes. Her skin was flawless, and surprisingly pale for someone who lived in a beach town in Florida. Or was it due to her recent illness?

He took another bite of the spicy taco salad and tried to banish his thoughts. He didn't care what she did or didn't do in Florida. As long as she didn't fly out of here in a huff like the last two temps, he'd be satisfied.

She brought in the faxed report, placing it near the plate on the desk.

He nodded, but she didn't leave. When he looked at her, she appeared nervous.

"Something wrong?" he asked.

"I don't think so." She cleared her throat, glanced down at the report, then met his eyes. "Your aunt invited us to stay here while I'm working for you. I asked her to recommend a place in town where we could live but she insisted we plan to remain here. I'm sure room and board aren't in the deal, so maybe you could recommend a place for us to look at in Tumbleweed. I could try to get something lined up this afternoon.''

He'd never thought about housing. Of course she had no place to stay in Texas, she was from Florida.

If she had to get a place in town, it would have to be furnished, inexpensive and without a lease. Nothing like that came to mind. There was the added worry about who would watch her son—especially after the surgery when Mitch was sure he'd have to be kept quiet for a while. Ginny Morgan knew no one in town. How would she keep her mind on business when a stranger was watching her convalescing child.

Emaline and Rosita would spoil the child in their delight to watch him.

''Staying here makes the most sense,'' he said. ''If you don't like the lilac room, ask Rosita to give you another.''

She looked at him as if he'd lost his mind.

''I can't stay here.''

He leaned back in his chair. ''Why not?''

''You're already doing so much. I can't take room and board as well.''

She certainly was not running some scam. He'd been around his fair share of proud, determined women. Marlisse had been very independent. Now this. Try to do a good deed and have to argue about it.

Do a good deed? Where had that come from? He was merely helping a child who needed it. It was easy to throw money at a problem. And he had it to spare. Not that it meant a thing. All the money in the world would not have saved Daisy or Marlisse.

Thinking about them usually brought their images to mind. But now he only saw Ginny.

"I have to read this report and draft a response. We'll need to get it faxed back today. Look for the Milford file. The temp couldn't find it or any of the others I asked for. How hard can it be?"

Ginny looked as if she wanted to argue the point of staying, but he had ended the discussion. She was smart enough to pick up on that.

Mitch relaxed slightly when she went to the file cabinets in her office and opened drawer after drawer. He could hear them slam shut. So the lady had a temper. She looked so sweet and young and feminine he hadn't expected that. She'd learned to control that temper somewhere, he hadn't picked up a clue until she slammed the drawers. What would it be like to let loose? Did that passionate feeling spill over into other areas? Like when she was involved with a man?

CHAPTER FOUR

BY DINNERTIME, Ginny's spirits were high. She'd worked a couple of hours in the office after lunch, arranged to visit the doctor with Joey the next afternoon and taken a nap at Emaline's insistence. She was feeling more resigned to staying at the Holden Ranch until Mitch's P.A. returned and falling in with Emaline's desires to watch Joey. She had mixed emotions—not wanting to be beholden to strangers, and grateful for the chance to have Joey's eyes operated on before she had thought possible.

She wished she had brought more than just a couple of changes of shorts and slacks, but hadn't expected to spend any more time with Joey's father than it took to have him meet Joey and get an agreement to help with the operation. Emaline always wore flowery dresses, which were a bit excessive, Ginny thought privately, but at least she dressed up for dinner. Ginny had to wear her same old slacks and shirt.

Still, Ginny's clothes were freshly laundered thanks to Rosita. And Joey was clean from a bath and a change of clothes.

When they entered the dining room, Emaline was already seated at the foot of the table.

"There you two are. Do sit. I thought one on either side, to balance the table. Mitch will be here soon. We'll began to eat once he arrives. I do hope you have an appetite tonight, Rosita has been cooking all afternoon. Did you sleep well, dear?'' she asked Ginny.

''The nap was lovely, thank you,'' Ginny responded, helping Joey into the indicated chair then going around the table to take her seat. The dining room was more formal than they were used to. Ginny hoped Joey's manners would hold up. Sometimes a four-year-old forgot.

Mitch entered at that moment, hesitating in the doorway as he looked at the three people already there. For a second, Ginny thought he might turn and leave. Should she have insisted on a tray in her room? He moved swiftly to the place at the table's head and sat, to her relief. She'd hate to be the cause of dissention in his household.

''I didn't realize we would all be eating together,'' he murmured with a look at his aunt.

''Now that Ginny's out of bed and feeling so much better, I knew you'd want us all to have our meals together. It's fine for Joey to eat with Rosita from time to time, but there's no need now that his mother is no longer sick. He needs to eat with family. I think Ginny looks in much better color, don't you? She was so pale that afternoon they arrived,'' Emaline said gaily. She was obviously pleased at the dinner arrangement.

Ginny felt warmth steal into her cheeks as Emaline continued. She darted a glance at Mitch to find his dark eyes studying her gravely as his aunt talked about Ginny's recovery. Her heart began to beat rapidly and she wondered if she'd made a mistake accepting this man's hospitality. She couldn't deny the spark of attraction she felt anytime she was in proximity to him. Not that she would let that influence her behavior. She was not looking for any kind of relationship. Been there, done that! Now, she had Joey to think about as well.

Rosita entered carrying bowls of vegetables and potatoes. Placing them in the center of the table, she returned in moments with a huge platter of fried chicken and a basket of fluffy biscuits.

Ginny remained feeling awkward after Mitch's comment. She hoped they could eat quickly and leave him in peace.

He ate without comment, as if as anxious to get finished and away from the table as she was. Tomorrow she'd suggest she and Joey eat in their room.

Emaline seemed to find nothing amiss with dinner and smiled at Joey as he worked his way through the dinner.

"Tell us what you did today, Joey," Emaline said. "I know we went to see the horses, but what else did you do?"

"Mr. Parlance said I could watch the cat in the barn and he let me pat the dogs, but I can't play with them because they're working dogs and he doesn't want them spoiled," Joey said solemnly.

"Oh pooh, those dogs know their jobs, a bit of fun with a little boy won't spoil them, will it Mitch?" Emaline said.

He glanced at her. "Jack handles that Emaline."

"But you could tell him to let Joey play with the dogs when they aren't working. Daisy did. A little boy needs to have a dog."

The tension at the table rose dramatically. Ginny

held her breath at the change, looking at Emaline in dismay. From the little she'd learned from the woman that morning, Mitch had taken his daughter's death hard and didn't speak of her. It almost seemed as if Emaline was pushing Ginny and Joey at Mitch—to replace his lost family. Ginny hoped she was misreading the situation. Nothing could be farther from her own reason for being here. If Emaline became too pushy, she and Joey would have to leave.

Mitch pushed back his chair and rose. "If you will excuse me." In two seconds he had left the room.

"Oh dear, I shouldn't have said that. Mitch is still so touchy about Marlisse and Daisy. But I wanted Joey to have the fun of playing with the dogs while he's here. Sophie is one of the dogs Daisy used to play with. I think they have a couple of new ones that she never saw. But it doesn't matter, the dogs wouldn't hurt the boy and he couldn't possibly untrain them." Emaline shook her head, staring after her nephew. "He acts as if Daisy and Marlisse never existed. I miss them, too. We all do. But I remember the good times, and wish I had someone to share them with," she said sadly.

Ginny knew staying would be impossible with the situation the way it was. Kind as Emaline had been, she couldn't remain. She'd have to find accommodation on her own, preferably before Mitch asked her to leave. She just hoped he'd let her keep the job. She couldn't bear it if he snatched that away just when she thought she could help Joey.

Once they had finished dinner, Ginny took Joey to his bedroom. "In the morning we're going to look for a nice apartment in Tumbleweed," she said, sink-ing on the edge of his bed. He had been given the rose room. She looked around, admiring the decorations, knowing a small boy would be happier with less things to knock against or stay away from.

"Can we get a dog?" he asked, leaning against her leg.

Ginny brushed back his light brown hair, and shook her head regretfully. "No, we won't be here that long. When we go back home, I'll see if the apartment manager will let us get a dog, how's that?"

"And a horse?"

Ginny laughed and hugged her son. "Not a horse. Goodness, it'll be crowded in our apartment with a dog, where would we put a horse?"

Joey laughed at her nonsense and offered several suggestions, each more outlandish than the other. Soon they were laughing together as they often did. Love surrounded them. Ginny savored the happy moment. She loved her son so much. How much of his life his father was missing. She wished she had found the man after searching so long.

When she put him to bed sometime later, she kissed him and tucked him in. "Sleep well, sweetie," she murmured, imagining how Mitch must feel having lost his little girl. For a moment, Ginny wanted to snatch Joey up and hold him tightly away from harm for the rest of their lives. The worst nightmare—losing a child. How did Mitch stand it?

She went back downstairs. The house was quiet. Lights were on in the living room and down the hall in the study. Ginny peered into both rooms, they were empty.

She turned to go back up stairs when something

had her push open the front door and step out into the wide veranda.

Mitch was sitting in one of the chairs on the right, his legs stretched out, hands tucked into the pockets of his pants. It was dark, only the light from the living room spilled out to provide illumination.

"Are you asleep?" she whispered. If he was, she'd tiptoe away.

"No." The short answer wasn't very conducive to conversation. But what she had to say couldn't be delayed.

She walked closer, leaning against a column, gazing over the dark landscape. The lights were on in the bunkhouse and the barn, otherwise the ranch was cocooned in the velvet night. Stars shone as pinpoints of lights in the vast expanse of the black sky.

"I apologize for the awkwardness at dinner," Ginny started. She wanted him to know it hadn't been her idea, without feeling she was trying to accuse Emaline.

"Aunt Emaline has the right to invite whomever she wishes to dinner," he commented.

"We're leaving in the morning."

"What are you talking about?" he asked, rising. In two steps he stood beside her.

Ginny looked up. His face was planes and shadows, but she knew he was staring down at her. Her breath caught in her throat, but she held firm.

"I'll still work for you, if that's what you want. And I'll be so grateful for the operation. I'll pay you back every cent."

"Not necessary."

"But we can't stay here, it isn't fair to you."

He was silent a long moment. "I can decide what is fair for me. Stay."

She shook her head. "I can't. We can't. It's too awkward, too painful."

"How?"

"I can see it in your eyes. You don't want Joey around, no children. Emaline said you disappear when your sister and her children come. You've asked your cousins not to come to visit. It's because of Daisy, I understand, truly I do, which is why we need to leave. That way you wouldn't be reminded, wouldn't have a rambunctious four-year-old underfoot all the time."

He turned and glared off into the night. The silence stretched out. Ginny wished she could do something to ease the man's anguish, but there was nothing. She was about to turn to reenter the house when he spoke, his voice low and pain fulled.

"She was eight. *Eight.* She should have had another eighty years!"

Ginny swallowed, longing to reach out and offer sympathy, not knowing if he would accept it. Words were so inadequate at a time like this.

"It's so tragic," she murmured. "I'm sorry. I wish I could do something to change things."

"A senseless waste of two good lives."

"I'm know." Tentatively she reached out to touch his arm. He turned, hesitated a moment. Even in the dim light, she could see the intensity of his gaze. He leaned closer and Ginny held her breath. Was he going to *kiss* her? Her heart raced. For the first time in years she longed for the touch of a man's mouth against hers. She had dated only casually since John Mitchell Holden had left her life. None of the men had interested her long enough for a second or third date.

But this attraction that flared had her wishing for things that couldn't be. She almost leaned forward, just a few scant inches, to meet him halfway. To offer her mouth to his, hoping he'd kiss her and find some solace in the contact.

Startled at the thought, Ginny did nothing for several minutes, conscious of the tension that rose until she could almost reach out and touch it.

Finally he turned with an expletive and headed out to toward the barn. Slowly she drew in a breath, unaware she'd been holding hers until he left.

She watched as he strode across the dark grass, his back ramrod straight and taut. He had wanted to kiss her, she was sure of it. And she had wanted him to.

Hadn't she learned anything from John Mitchell Holden of Ft. Lauderdale? Shivering with the closeness of the contact, she turn and fled into the house, afraid of the sensations that filled her, of the yearning for that one man that filled her. She had no business thinking of anything between them except business—and then only as a way to repay the magnificent gift he was giving her.

"Blame it on the night and the company and the memories," she tried to tell herself as she got ready for bed. "He's a man, you're a woman, it was proximity, or the romantic feel to the night. He wasn't going to kiss you personally, just any woman to try to forget the pain he lived with every day. Men don't feel the same emotional tie as women," she reminded herself.

When she slipped between the sheets of her bed,

she tried to convince herself. But a part of her still craved a kiss from Mitch Holden.

"No harm done," she said. No harm? Maybe not, but for a brief moment she'd felt she was in reach of paradise. It made her sad to know it meant nothing to Mitch. And that it would not happen again.

Mitch heard the door shut from the corral. He leaned against the top rail and watched the horses resting for the night. The silence was deafening. What had he been thinking, trying to find relief from the constant ache of Marlisse's passing, of Daisy's death by kissing a stranger? He wasn't into such activities. He hadn't been with a woman since Marlisse. Hadn't kissed anyone since her death. He certainly had no business thinking of Ginny that way.

He rubbed his face with both hands, and shook his head in disgust. If her reasons for leaving hadn't already been strong enough, he'd just made sure she had a few more. She was a guest on the property, deserving of his care and protection. Not have to worry she'd have to fight off his advances.

He slammed the heel of his hand against the post startling the horses. He couldn't deny the feelings in his gut—the desire he had for closeness, for a woman's touch. But it also felt like a betrayal to Marlisse. Dammit, why had Ginny stumbled onto his ranch. And who had been impersonating him five years ago?

Getting no answers, he turned and headed for the office. He'd get some work done, try to forget the way his life was going by reviewing every bit of information he had on the Hollister situation. And just maybe tomorrow he'd head for Los Angeles and take care of things himself.

He certainly couldn't make a bigger mess of that situation than he had with Ginny Morgan and her son.

By the time dawn broke on the horizon, Mitch had consumed three pots of coffee, found a glitch they'd overlooked on the Hollister deal, and was dog tired. He left a batch of faxes for Ginny to send.

Before showering for the day, he'd take a ride to clear his head. And decide just how much he was willing to unbend to keep his temporary assistant and her son on the ranch. Maybe it would be best for them to find accommodations in town.

But he knew he couldn't have her that far away.

Saddling his favorite horse, Mitch was soon heading away from the main barn. As he passed the house, he glanced at the room Ginny slept in. For a moment he could swear he could feel her slim body against his. Would she be soft and sweet, her womanly curves fitted against his own, harder body? He spurred the horse, trying to quell the image that wouldn't go away.

When Ginny entered the kitchen sometime later, she was surprised to see Joey already dressed and eating breakfast.

"I didn't hear you get up," she said, leaning over to give him a kiss on his cheek as he shoveled cereal into his mouth.

"Hi Mommy. I was hungry."

"I can prepare you a tray, Miss Morgan," Rosita said, turning from the stove.

"Could I just eat here? With Joey?" Ginny asked.

She wasn't sure of the protocol, but breakfast would be very comfortable in the sun-filled room and she wanted to spend time with her son, rather than in isolation in her room.

"Certainly. What would you like this morning? I have eggs ready to go, sausages warming, biscuits, and grits."

"All of the above," Ginny said, slipping into the seat next to Joey. She was starving—must be from not eating much over the last few days.

"Maybe you can help me, Rosita. I need to find an inexpensive place to stay in Tumbleweed while we're here. But I don't want a lease. We'll only be here long enough for Joey to have his operation and until Helen returns."

Rosita frowned. "I thought you were staying here in the house. Miss Emaline told me so yesterday."

"I think it best if we stay in town."

Rosita raised her eyebrow in question. "It is not extra work for me," she said slowly. "This is a big house, it is nice to have more rooms in use, more people to look after. Sometimes I have little to do."

Ginny looked at Joey, then back to Rosita. "I think it's not as nice for Mitch. We're invading his privacy, forcing him into situations he'd just as soon avoid."

"Ah." The older woman nodded gravely. "Perhaps because of the child, but time moves on. Maybe you and the boy are what Señor Holden needs to help him move on as well."

"He's already doing so much for us, I hate to make things awkward," Ginny said.

"I'll give you the address for my friend Samantha Billing. She works in the real estate office in town. If there are any short-term rentals, she'll know of them. But you must check with Señor Holden first.''

"Thank you. I'm sure he'll have no problem with you giving me your friend's address." Glad to have that settled, Ginny ate quickly, asking Joey how he got himself dressed.

"Aunt Emaline said a big boy like me could probably do it all by myself and I did when you were sick! Now I can do it every day," he said proudly.

So that was who took care of him while she'd been out of it. She'd wondered if it had been Emaline or Rosita. Both women seem happy to have Joey around. She only hoped they were up to his endless energy.

Bracing herself when she entered the office a little later, Ginny was momentarily disappointed to find Mitch hadn't arrived. Or had he? There was a pile of papers on her desk, with cryptic notes attached to two stacks, and a separate note for her. With her work outlined, she had plenty to do without confronting the man after last night.

Ginny felt a warmth invade her heart when she saw the first item on the note to her was he would be back by the time she needed to leave for the doctor's appointment he'd arranged. He hadn't forgotten, but she had. No looking for an apartment today.

It took more than ten minutes for her to figure out how to use the fax machine, but Ginny kept trying different buttons and sequences until the paper she'd stacked in the bin began feeding through. In the meantime, the phone rang several times. Buoyed up by her success yesterday, she soon felt confident in not disconnecting people, and in getting the messages down as clearly as she could.

Mitch strode into the room as the last page of the second fax was feeding through. For a moment Ginny felt a flare of panic. Should she say something about last night or ignore it? After all, nothing had really happened. It only felt like her life had been on the edge of a precipice and she wasn't sure if she had fallen or not.

"Good morning," he said.

"Good morning." Her heart fluttered and she knew color rose in her cheeks. She had always hated how that happened. Would she never outgrow that childish reaction? He didn't seem to notice, however, striding quickly through the outer office into his own.

He left the door open, and Ginny watched him sit behind the desk. He and Helen probably set the office up so they could talk back and forth if needed.

The phone rang again and she answered. "It's for you, a Joel Brady," she called.

She turned back to the files he'd left on her desk. She'd put them away and see what else he wanted done. He had mentioned yesterday he was sending dictation tapes into the office in Dallas for his secretary there to transcribe.

When the phone rang again, she picked it up, noticing Mitch was still on the first call.

"This is Harry in L.A. Tell Mitch I've heard of being cryptic before, but to fax eleven pages of blank paper is a bit over the top. What am I supposed to do with this?"

"Blank? But there was writing on every sheet," she said, looking at the stack in front of her. "Who is this?"

"Harry in Los Angeles. This isn't Helen, is it? Where's Helen?"

"She's away. I'm filling in." And not doing a very good job, Ginny thought guiltily. She looked at the two stacks. One had only five sheets, so she knew instantly which stack she'd have to resend. "I'm new at this. I thought I sent the fax through, each page went through the machine."

"Nothing came through. Did you have the pages backward in the feeder? Try flipping them over. Send again."

"I'll resend right away."

"Fine. Have Mitch call me when he's free."

Ginny quickly resent the fax, flipping the pages. She wanted to do a good job to justify Mitch's helping her with the operation, but she felt foolish not being able to handle a simple thing like sending a fax. With such incompetence, would he reconsider her working for him?

She wrote up the message and added the pink note to the growing stack. How did he have time to talk to all these people every day and still get other work done?

She looked up from her work and studied the man. He seemed tired, though he was still immaculately turned out. He glanced up just then and caught her gaze, holding it a full minute. Ginny's heart began to pound. She felt fluttery, awareness rose just as it had last night.

It was after eleven when Ginny tidied her desk in preparation for leaving. Through Mitch's Dallas office an appointment had been made with the specialist at two o'clock in downtown Dallas. Ginny wanted plenty of time to locate the doctor's offices.

Mitch hung up the phone and walked out to the outer office, checking his watch.

"We should be leaving soon. We can grab a bite of lunch on the way."

"What?" Was she missing something? Where was Mitch going?

"I'm driving you and Joey into Dallas."

Ginny was nonplussed. "I can manage. You have work to do." Besides, she almost added, you want nothing to do with my child, or any child, you've made that clear.

"I worked last night, caught up on everything important. The phone calls can wait. I'll drop you off, pick you up when you're ready to leave. Jed said the exam and tests would take about two hours. I'll stop by the Dallas office while you are at the doctor's."

"I don't know what to say. Thank you!" His driving would mean she didn't have to chance her old car, didn't have to figure out where to go in a strange city, didn't have to worry about parking. It also meant she could devote her attention to Joey if he became nervous or upset. She was grateful to Mitch for his offer.

Even more grateful when she was settled in the front seat of the luxury sedan he drove. The environmental control kept the temperature cool in the humid heat, the tinted windows made it easier to watch the unfolding scenery as they sped quickly toward the city. The sun shone in a cloudless sky. It was such a difference from the rainy day she'd arrived, she took advantage to watch the landscape as it flew by.

Joey had brought one of his books and was buckled into his car seat, happy to look at the pictures.

Ginny knew it would take a while to reach Dallas, was she supposed to keep quiet or make small talk? She fidgeted with her purse strap, uncertain how to behave. Normally she was friendly and found it easy to talk with people, but Mitch was different.

"How far from the doctor's are your Dallas offices?" she finally asked, the silence too much to bear.

"Only a few blocks. I'll give you the office phone number, if you finish earlier than anticipated, call me. I can be there quickly."

"We could walk to the offices, give us a chance to see something of Dallas."

"No need. It's going to be hot, and your son would probably wilt in the heat."

"His name is Joey," she said, wondering if she'd ever heard Mitch call him by name.

"Joey. He's five?"

"He'll be five his next birthday, but he's only four right now."

"Tall for his age."

"His father was tall."

Mitch flicked her a quick glance. "Must be tough, raising a child on your own."

"It has its rewards," she murmured. It had it drawbacks as well, which is why she'd been trying to find Joey's father since she'd first found out she was pregnant. All children should have both parents—even if they didn't live together. But she had never found the man she'd searched for over the years.

"How old are you?"

"Twenty-three."

Mitch looked startled. "That young?"

"How old did you think I was?"

"Older, though you don't look it. You were eighteen when you got pregnant?"

"Seventeen, almost eighteen."

He uttered an expletive. "What was the guy thinking?"

She sighed. "In retrospect, I suspect he wasn't thinking at all, just out to have fun. Spring break is wild in Fort Lauderdale."

"How did you meet him?"

Ginny wondered why all the questions. Had the quietness of the drive bothered him as well? She doubted it—nothing seemed to bother Mitch Holden.

"I was waiting tables for some extra money. I was a senior in high school and wanted a particular dress for the prom. I had to earn the money myself."

"Parents couldn't help? Or at least warn you about randy college guys?"

"My parents died when I was eight. I lived with my Aunt Edith, who did warn me, time and time again. But I thought I was in love. I'd never felt like that before. And he was very—attentive, I guess. It wasn't until he left I realized it had been only a fling on his part."

"After you knew you were pregnant?"

"I tried to find him. But never could."

"Until you saw the article."

"Yes, though I still haven't found my John Mitchell Holden. You are nothing like him. Older for one thing."

And eons more mature. He had a presence that

other men would envy. And probably had women yearning after him like love struck teenagers. It was a good thing she was immune to his attraction. She would not be caught fantasizing a second time about romance and happy ever after. Reality was hard, and Ginny had learned that lesson well.

"Did you try private investigators?"

She laughed softly. "We didn't have that kind of money. I did consider giving him up," she said softly, so her son wouldn't hear her. "But I just couldn't. Aunt Edith was not keen on my keeping the baby, but she ended up being a terrific help. She loved him to bits."

"Past tense?"

"She died two years ago in a freak accident. A bus jumped the curb, slamming into several people waiting. She and another were killed, three more were badly injured. I miss her a lot." What an understatement. Ginny had lost her mainstay when her aunt had died. But she had no choice but to move on, she had her son to care for.

"So it's just you and Joey?"

Ginny nodded, pleased he'd said her son's name easily enough this time.

"So I do know what it's like to lose someone you love," she added softly. "Life eventually moves on."

"Two someone's it sounds like, your aunt, and Joey's father."

"I guess," she said.

Mitch flicked a glance her way. She was gazing out the window, apparently lost in thought. Thinking about Joey's father? How could the man have disappeared without considering the consequences of his actions. Did she still miss him with the intensity he missed Marlisse.

Maybe he and Ginny had something in common. The other man wasn't in the picture, but he was. He frowned. Not that it meant anything. But he couldn't help feeling protective toward her. She had come up against terrific odds, yet seemed content in her life, plunging ahead with courage he admired. She hadn't asked for anything from anyone.

Yet she never gave up hope of finding Joey's father. Was there anything he could do? Hire those private investigators she couldn't afford?

As the traffic grew heavier, Mitch tried to ignore the spark of protectiveness that rose. He didn't owe Ginny or her son anything. The best thing would be to step back, distance himself from them and their situation before they grew to depend upon him. He knew that way lay danger.

He hadn't been able to keep his wife and child safe.

He could help a little, just enough to make things easier—not become involved.

When Mitch dropped Ginny and Joey off at the high-rise building which housed the doctor's office, he handed her his business card. "Remember to call if you get out early, otherwise, I'll be here at four."

"Thanks." She gripped Joey's hand and headed into the building without a backward glance. Mitch ignored the urge to follow them, to be with her while she waited for the tests. He had work to do, and nothing to offer his uninvited guests.

At four exactly, Ginny and Joey walked out onto the hot sidewalk. Her head was spinning.

"There's Mitch!" Joey said excitedly pointing to the car parked at the curb part way down the block.

"You should call him Mr. Holden," she admonished following his finger and spotting the car. She held his hand tightly as they hurried toward it.

"Aunt Emaline calls him Mitch. So do you, I've heard you."

"Unless he asks you to use his first name, it's more polite for a little boy to use a person's last name." She opened the back door and fastened him in his car seat, then slid into her place in the front. She felt a bit shaky and relished the comfort of the soft seats.

"How did it go?" Mitch asked, not yet moving from their spot.

Dazed, Ginny looked at him. "They can do the procedure on Friday and if it all goes well, he'll be able to go home on Monday. The bandages will remain for a couple of weeks, though, and he has to keep quiet, no running around." She couldn't believe things were happening so swiftly. She knew it was due to Mitch and his influence. Gratitude rose. "Thank you. I never thought we'd have it done so soon!"

"That's good, then," Mitch said. Jed had come through. Mitch had told him to pull any strings he could to expedite the procedure.

Ginny simply smiled as she nodded, tears filling her eyes. "It's terrific. I can't thank you enough."

He frowned and started the car, pulling out into traffic before speaking again. "No thanks needed. You're the first one who didn't dash out of the office the minute I complained about something, or yelled about a missing file. At least I have help until Helen returns.''

Ginny nodded, blinking away the tears. To her it was a wonderful gift. To Mitch it was merely an exchange for someone to help in his office at home.

But, couldn't he have had one of the women from the Dallas office drive out every day?

CHAPTER FIVE

Mitch glanced again at the glow in Ginny's eyes and felt as if she'd touched him. For the first time in years he forgot the past and remained in the present. Beginning to enjoy her wonder and delight, he frowned, not wanting to get caught up in that illusion of happiness. Life had a way of slapping one down just when things were looking up.

"I can't believe after all this time it's really going to happen," she said again. "He will have to be calm and not do any leaning over for a month or so after the surgery. But then, everything should be healed and he'll be as normal as you or I."

"As every child should." As Daisy had been, with her bright eyes and ready laughter. Daisy would have liked showing her pony and the dogs to Joey. She'd been such an outgoing child.

"I can't express how much I appreciate your paying for this. I'll pay you back, every cent!"

"You're earning it working for me. There will be no debt." Mitch said no more, concentrating on traffic. He glanced in the rearview mirror—the little boy was asleep, tilted sideways in the car seat. Joey. How could any man father such an adorable child and not want to acknowledge him? Maybe he'd see what he could do in locating the man. See the happiness in Ginny's eyes again.

Of course, Joey's father didn't know of his existence.

Once again Mitch tried to picture someone using his name. It sounded like someone that knew him and the ranch, from what Ginny had said. Yet he could not come up with anyone he knew with blond hair and blue eyes who was the right age to be Joey's father.

Ginny was resting her head on the back of the seat. Had she fallen asleep, too?

When she stirred, he took the chance she was awake.

"Tell me more about Joey's father. I'm still trying to figure out who would have used my name."

"I've pretty much told you all I remember. He was so much fun, swept me off my feet. He was tall and athletic. He could swim like a fish and loved to body surf. He wore sunglasses a lot, maybe to hide his eyes, but I didn't think so at the time. They were as blue as Joey's."

"He was blond you said."

"Yes. About six feet two or so. He had a high opinion of himself—which I shared until he left."

"What did you do after that?" It wasn't like him to ask questions of strangers. She'd work for him until Helen came back, then return to Florida. They were not going to remain in contact once she left. Yet he wanted to know more about her, know every thing that happened to her. Try to get a handle on the woman who had overcome such hardships and come out with such an optimistic view of life.

"I finished high school before I realized I was pregnant. College was out of the questions once I decided to keep Joey. Aunt Edith helped out, and I went full-time at the Shrimp Shack.''

"What did you want to study in college?''

She looked at him a moment as if weighing his reaction to her reply. "Architecture.''

That startled him. "Shopping malls and office complexes?''

"No, family homes. I've never lived in one and thought it would be so great to design homes for families of all sizes. There's such a wide variety of architectural styles for houses, from very modern, to reproductions of Victorian, to old-fashioned farmhouses. Depending on the building lot and the lifestyle of the people who would live in it, I thought I could design the perfect home for each customer.''

"You could still go to college and get that degree.''

"Maybe, once Joey's in school. In the meantime, I have enough to do with Joey and work.''

He wondered how she managed on a waitress' salary. It had to be difficult, yet she had never complained, nor even hinted he might help her out financially. Was that coming later? Would she find reasons to stay in Texas, reasons to try to get him to finance her new lifestyle? He doubted it. It would be easier if she did.

Dinner with everyone at the table that evening was more relaxed than the night before. Mitch was tired—not having slept for two days was beginning to make its impact. He ate Rosita's delicious cooking, trying to distance himself from the others at the table. But despite his best efforts, he was intrigued with Ginny Morgan. Her eyes sparkled when she told Emaline about the Friday surgery date. She laughed at something Joey said, her cheeks flushed with warmth, her eyes full of love.

He wanted to touch that soft hair, brush it back from her face and cradle her head in his hands holding her for a kiss, not cut and run like a scared rabbit. But a kiss that would make him forget the past and open the door to something new. It had been a long time since he'd kissed anyone, but he wanted Ginny.

"I'll go with you to the hospital on Friday," Emaline said.

"You don't have to do that. We have to be there at six in the morning. I figured I'd have to leave around 4:30 a.m. to make it on time," Ginny said.

"You'll want someone with you while you're waiting. I'm not so old I can't get up early once in a while, young lady!"

"Thank you, Emaline, I'll be grateful for your support."

Emaline looked at Mitch. "Will you be going with us?"

Mitch shook his head, catching the disappointed look on Joey's face. "Tomorrow and Friday I'll be out with the cattle. We've delayed moving the major portion of the herd as it is because of the late rain and the muddy fields."

"The men can handle it," Emaline said primly. "You should be with us."

Mitch hated hospitals. Hadn't he heard the worst news of his life in one? Even the thought of entering another had him tensing. Ginny didn't need him. If she'd stayed in Florida, when the operation had come, she would have been alone.

He didn't like the thought.

"We'll manage fine. I couldn't ask Mitch to skip a day of work for us. It's bad enough I'm missing a day when I just started," Ginny said firmly. "We'll drive in early and have breakfast there once Joey's settled."

Mitch had visions of her old car breaking down in the predawn morning, stalling on the highway, of someone not seeing it and slamming into it in the dark.

"Take my car," he said abruptly.

"What?"

"It'll be more reliable than yours."

Ginny bristled. "My car is perfectly fine, thank you very much."

Mitch said nothing, but he would make sure she took a more reliable vehicle than that old one of hers. He couldn't dispel the image of a fiery crash.

After dinner, Ginny bathed Joey and talked to him about the upcoming surgery. The doctor had given them a little book designed to explain things to young children. She was getting ready to tuck him into bed when Mitch appeared.

"Hi Mr. Holden," Joey called from his bed. "Did you come to tuck me in, too?"

For a moment Mitch relived the bedtime ritual he'd had with Daisy. Both he and Marlisse tried to be with her when time for bed, reading her a story, talking about her day, and tucking her into bed.

The little boy looked hopeful as he smiled at Mitch.

"I came to talk to your mother when she's finished here," he said gruffly.

"Oh." The disappointment was almost tangible.

"But now that Mitch is here, he can help me tuck

you in, can't you?'' Ginny's glare clearly conveyed her message—help or else!

Mitch stepped inside and crossed to the bed. ''Good night,'' he said.

''You have to tuck in the covers,'' Joey said.

Mitch pulled the covers taut, tucking them around Joey. ''Sleep well,'' he said, stepping back.

Ginny kissed her son and hugged him. ''Tomorrow you can tell Mr. Parlance all about your operation.''

''And about getting ice cream when I'm good for the operation,'' Joey added.

''That's right. I love you, Joey,'' she said, kissing him again.

''Night Mommy. Night Mr. Holden.''

''Call me Mitch,'' Mitch said. Might as well, the longer name was a mouthful for a little kid.

When they closed the door to the room behind them, Ginny turned. ''What did you want to see me about?'' she asked. He was too close. She could feel the heat of his body envelop her. Was he deliberately invading her space? Slowly she took a step backward to a safer distance. She almost laughed. He hadn't kissed her last night, and she doubted he had any plans in that direction tonight. She was letting her imagination take flight.

He didn't seem to be aware of her discomfort or crazy thoughts. Not about the kiss and not about the fact she wanted to fling herself into his arms and have him tell her everything would be all right. No one could guarantee that. And he'd probably think her certifiably crazy if she did so.

''I wanted to discuss a few things about work. How

about we go out on the veranda. The evening is still warm,'' he suggested.

She nodded, her heart skipping a beat. It had been on the veranda he'd almost kissed her. Hadn't he? Not that she would encourage that kind of thing even if he were interested. Ginny knew her stay was temporary. She had no more illusions about love and marriage and happy ever after. She'd thought she was in love with the boy she'd met at spring break, but as time had passed, she realized she'd been in love with the illusion of love. With the fantasy of devotion and fun and desire. They had little in common—like honesty and reliability. She knew so little about the man who had fathered Joey.

She'd grown since then. She was more mature, and more discerning. She wanted a lot more than a casual fling, no matter how appealing it might be with Mitch.

He gestured toward the rockers to the right of the front door and Ginny sat in one. She had a view of the rolling hills, fading to black as the night came down. From the bunkhouse, she could hear the murmur of voices. Once in a while a man laughed.

Mitch sat in the chair beside her, as he'd been last night when she'd found him.

''I'll be going up with the herd tomorrow and we won't be back until late. If Stevenson calls, refer him to Hank in the Dallas office. I don't expect any major problems, but if they arise, I'll carry my cell phone. Call if there's an emergency.''

''Otherwise, I'll tell everyone you'll call them back on Monday?''

''I'll be back in the late afternoon, still time to call L.A. if needed. But handle what you can yourself.

Activate the answering machine at the end of the day. It can take messages Friday."

"Me field your calls? I don't know anything about what you're doing! I'm lucky not to disconnect callers anymore."

"You pick up things faster than the two temps from the agency in town did."

Ginny felt a warm glow at his halfhearted compliment. She'd been doing her best in an alien environment. It was nothing like waiting tables. She was happy to hear it wasn't all in vain.

"About Friday," Mitch began.

"My car will work," she said stubbornly.

"My car would be more comfortable for Aunt Emaline," he replied quickly.

She looked at him in the growing darkness. She hadn't considered Emaline. Was she letting foolish pride stand in her way? The older woman was coming to help her out. Maybe she should take his blasted car and stop arguing.

"I hadn't thought about that," she murmured.

"Think about it."

"It's bigger than what I'm used to."

"I could have one of the men drive you in. But I need them for the cattle. When will you be ready to return?"

"I don't know. After Joey goes to sleep, I guess. Do you think Emaline would stay that long? Maybe she shouldn't go with us after all. It could be a long day. I can get a hotel room nearby."

"She wants to go. Let her. She'll talk your ear off and make you forget your worries for a while. And

I'm the last one to suggest she will get tired. She'd set me in my place fast.''

''Does she do that to you?'' Ginny asked softly, trying to imagine his delicate aunt talking endlessly and Mitch just sitting and listening. ''Talk your ear off?''

''Sometimes.''

''I bet she tells you wonderful things about Daisy,'' she said slowly.

''We don't talk about Daisy around here,'' he said heavily.

''Why ever not? I'd want to talk about Joey all the time, to make sure everyone remembered him. To celebrate his life. To remember the great times together.'' Ginny had heard Emaline when she mentioned Mitch never talked about Daisy, but she didn't understand it.

''Memories can be painful,'' Mitch said slowly.

''Yes. I know because I've really missed Aunt Edith since she died. But now I can laugh at some of the memories of things we did. I always feel a poignant longing to go back to the way things were when Joey was an infant, or even before when it was just Aunt Edith and me. But I know I can't. So I do what I can to celebrate her life. She was so special to me. She raised me after my folks died. That couldn't have been easy. She never married, was in her fifties when I came to live with her. Yet she loved me and later Joey like we were always her own.''

Impulsively, Ginny reached out and grabbed Mitch's hand. ''Tell me one special memory you have of Daisy.'' Her aunt was one who always *did*. Maybe

Mitch needed to do something, even if only to recall one special event in his daughter's life.

His fingers tightened on hers, but he remained silent for a long time. Finally, he began to speak, "The first time I took her up with me on a horse. We rode to the river and back. She held on to the reins, and I let her think she was directing the horse. She laughed and yelled and slapped those reins on the horse's neck. Her soft baby hair blew up into my face. Marlisse didn't cut it until she started school, so at age three it was long and fine and smelled like baby girl. She laughed the entire way, delighting in being up on a big horse with her daddy."

Ginny could envision the happiness the day must have held. She knew the little girl had lack for nothing in this family. Love spilled out with every word Mitch said. She wished for a moment Mitch had been Joey's father. What a wonderful father he must have been.

"Tell me all about her, what color was her hair? Did she like vegetables? What was her favorite song?" Ginny urged.

Slowly at first, then more easily he opened up. For two hours Mitch talked about his little girl. Marlisse figured prominently in many of the scenarios he recounted and Ginny drew a mental image of the close-knit, loving family. How doubly tragic it all ended so soon.

When Mitch stopped, she realized he still held her hand. She had never felt closer to another person, except Aunt Edith, than she did Mitch Holden at this moment. The night was quiet around them. The air had cooled, but not uncomfortably so. The stars were brilliant points of glittering light in the black velvet sky.

Not wanting to break the mood, Ginny didn't know how to leave. She felt as if she'd been given a very precious gift, made even more special coming from Mitch.

He solved her problem.

"God, I'm tried. I'd better head for bed. We leave at first light in the morning." His voice was gruff.

"Thanks for telling me about Daisy," she said softly, rising when he did.

He released her hand, but caught her shoulders in a light hold. "You're a dangerous woman, Ginny Morgan. I haven't talked about Daisy since her death. I had almost forgotten all those special times."

"But didn't you have fun tonight remembering how special she was. I know it hurts to have her gone, but you have such wonderful memories. I believe she was truly a happy child her entire life."

"You've given me the gift of my daughter again. Thank you." He drew her closer and kissed her.

Ginny was not prepared for a kiss. The sensations that swept through her caught her unaware, then flared into bright heat. His mouth was warm and enticing. The kiss was the most exciting thing she'd ever experienced. When he parted her lips with his tongue, she felt a warmth wash through her hotter than the Texas sun. Her legs felt weak and she hoped she wouldn't melt into a puddle at his feet. Twining her arms around his neck, she gave back as good as she got, relishing every heartbeat, every inch of his body pressed against hers. She savored the feel of her soft body against his harder one. She had never felt such a connection, such a feeling of wonder and rightness.

He deepened the kiss and she forgot about gratitude and lost children and feeling alive, and relished every magical moment when her life seemed to be spinning to the heavens. He kissed her as no man ever had, and she delighted in every stolen moment.

When he slowly eased back, she felt bereft. She didn't want to stop. They could have kissed all night and it would end too soon. But he was her boss. The man who was helping her with her son's expenses for the operation, not someone to fantasize about. A kiss to thank her for rekindling memories, that was all. She'd do best to keep that firmly in mind! She wouldn't be fooled a second time by a man's attention. She had her life charted, and side trips into sexual fantasy wasn't on the map.

"I'll take good care of the office tomorrow," she said breathlessly, then turned and fled for the safety of her room.

She was getting in over her head with Mitch Holden. Hadn't she learned from her prior experience? This was not some courtship leading to happy ever after. At least the man she'd known in Fort Lauderdale had pretended, Mitch had never given her a morsel of hope. She had better remember that every moment she remained on the Holden ranch!

Ginny found the office flat with Mitch gone. She fielded telephone calls, received faxed reports which she promptly placed on his desk, and finished the filing. She was proud he had left her to her own devices.

She wasn't the secretary he was used to, but she was coping.

Joey came to see her shortly before lunch and she let him play on the computer until she took her lunch break.

The afternoon seemed to drag. She read some of the reports that had come in, but they confused her. She didn't understand all that was going on, but she knew Mitch was a key player in several large corporations, as well as the boss of the family ranch.

Just before Ginny was about to call it a day and close up, a flashy red sports utility vehicle drove up and parked right in front of the office. A tall, slim young woman exited, glanced around and headed into the office. Her dark hair spilled down in a glossy waterfall across her shoulders. Her makeup was flawless. Her shirt looked tailored and her designer jeans looked brand new topping polished snakeskin boots. Ginny was instantly aware of the differences between the two of them—her off the rack jeans and shirt, no makeup and who knew what her hair looked like.

"Mitch around?" she drawled eyeing Ginny like she was an alien.

"He's out on the range today," Ginny said politely. She knew how to deal with the public—even people she didn't like. And this person was definitely not destined to become her best friend.

"I can tell Mitch you stopped by, shall I, Miss?"

"Gloria Devon." She wandered to the door of Mitch's office and looked in.

Ginny wondered if Gloria didn't believe her and was checking for herself. Did she and Mitch have a friendship that allowed her to wander into his office?

Not knowing, Ginny would rather err on the side of caution. She rose and moved swiftly to the door beside Gloria. As far as Ginny knew, Gloria had no business going into Mitch's private office and if she stepped one foot inside—

Gloria turned and walked back to Ginny's desk, sitting carelessly on one corner and studying Ginny.

"I heard from Emaline that Mitch had someone taking Helen's place until she returns. I live on the adjacent ranch. Mitch and I are close friends. Very close friends. Have you heard when Helen's coming back?"

Ginny blinked, feeling a twinge of jealousy. Mitch had kissed her last night, but was close with this woman? Of course their kiss had meant nothing, why would he ever look at her when he had a relationship with this beauty? Even more reason to keep a tight rein on her emotions. The lecture she'd given herself last night rose and she reminded herself to repeat it at every opportunity. Mitch Holden was not for her!

"I haven't spoken with Helen. I don't know what she's told Mitch," Ginny said, feeling at a loss. Despite everything, she had loved the kiss, and woven fantasies around it. Now they vanished as in a puff of smoke. Once again reality was staring her in the face.

"I could have helped Mitch around here. He should have asked me," Gloria said, glancing around the office. "Let him know I'm available, will you?"

Ginny wisely kept silent. She would not be drawn into a discussion with this stranger over the actions of her boss. Her loyalty lay with Mitch. And she couldn't help thinking once he knew Gloria was available her time as office assistant would be limited.

Gloria stood and glanced around once more as if trying to discover something that would keep her longer. Finding nothing, she shrugged. "Tell Mitch to give me a call. There's a barbecue tomorrow night at Ted Sampson's place. I thought Mitch could take me."

"I don't think so," Mitch replied from the doorway.

Ginny leaned to one side so she could see around Gloria. He walked in, slapping a dusty hat against equally dusty jeans. He looked hard, tired, dirty—and wonderful. Ginny didn't know if she was up to watching Gloria and Mitch interact, not that she had any choice in the matter. How did such close friends greet each other—with no holds barred, or more discretely?

"Hi, Mitch!" Gloria greeted him enthusiastically, going over as if to give him a hug.

He stepped back, holding up his hand. "I'm dusty and sweaty. What are you doing here, Gloria?"

"Like I was telling your new little secretary, Ted is throwing a barbecue tomorrow night. I'm sure you got an invitation. Since we live so close, I thought we could go over together. That way I wouldn't have to worry about driving back home all by my lonesome after dark." Her flirtatious look spoke volumes.

Oh, please, Ginny thought. Anyone more capable she'd never seen. She suspected Gloria never gave a thought to driving anywhere by herself no matter what the time of day or night! Why not come out and tell the man she wanted him to take her because of their involvement. Or were they keeping it a secret for some reason? Whatever, Ginny didn't want to stand and watch.

"Isn't your father going?" Mitch asked.

"No, he's in El Paso, won't be home until next week sometime. Come on, Mitch. It'll be fun to see all your neighbors and enjoy yourself a bit. You are such a hermit these days."

Ginny waited for him to blast her for treading on sensitive turf, but he merely shook his head.

"No can do, Gloria. I already have plans."

"What plans?"

"I'm taking Ginny to Dallas tomorrow. Her son is having surgery and I need to be there."

CHAPTER SIX

GINNY almost dropped her jaw. Mitch was telling Gloria he needed to be with her when Joey had his surgery? She was stunned. Though not as surprised as Gloria seemed when she spun around to glare at Ginny.

"You're going to the hospital with her? She has a child and you're involved? What happened to your famous vow to stay away from entanglements and from all children?" she asked, hands on hips glaring at Mitch.

Ginny felt a small spurt of pleasure to see the anger on the woman's face. She studied Mitch. He didn't seem too perturbed to have Gloria angry at him.

"I've been waiting for two years for you to loosen up a little. Here's a perfect opportunity to get back in the swing of things, and you're going to some damn hospital?" Gloria almost shouted.

"I don't know what you mean about waiting, but I'm driving Ginny in tomorrow morning early and I don't know when we'll be back—not tomorrow night. We're staying in a hotel in town close to the hospital," Mitch said, his eyes narrowed as he regarded his neighbor warily.

If looks could injure, Gloria's venomous expression would have shriveled Ginny right up.

She wanted to protest she knew nothing about Mitch's plans, but loyalty kept her quiet. And curiosity. What was he doing telling her such a tall tale? Emaline was going with her. Granted, they had already discussed staying at the hotel closest to the hospital together, but no mention of Mitch had been made. Ginny thought he was needed with the cattle or roundup or something.

"Call me when you finish playing nursemaid," Gloria said, stalking out. They heard the car door slam. When the wheels spun and squealed, Ginny dared a glance at Mitch. He was watching her.

"She has a bit of a temper," he said.

Wisely, Ginny decided not to respond to that. "I didn't expect you back until later."

"My horse threw a shoe. We didn't have a replacement with us, so I brought him in to have it fixed."

She purposely didn't bring up his startling comment that he was going into Dallas with her, but she wanted to. Would he? Or was that just an excuse for the pushy Gloria? What was their relationship. Not that it mattered, Ginny tried to convince herself. She and Mitch were not involved!

"Anything crucial? Or do I have time to go get cleaned up before dinner?" he asked.

"There were two phone calls that I referred to the Dallas office. The rest said they could wait until Monday. Hank sent you a long fax, and you got two others that were single sheets." She couldn't contain her curiosity any longer. "Did you mean it when you said you are driving us into Dallas, or was that just an excuse for Gloria?"

"I meant it." He turned and headed toward the house to shower and change before dinner.

Ginny watched him walk away. Had something

happened she didn't know about? Why was he involving himself in her problem after saying he wanted to keep his distance? Emaline said he never participated in family events anymore. Why would he do something for her—a stranger?

Gloria had been right, from what had happened to his family, helping Ginny out would be the last thing he'd want to do. Yet she was sure she had just heard him say he was accompanying them tomorrow.

Emaline was surprised as Ginny to learn of Mitch's change of plans. She had reserved a suite at the hotel closest to the hospital, thinking she and Ginny would need some time and space to be rested for Joey. But if Mitch accompanied them, they'd have to share the suite—or he'd have to get his own room. She watched Mitch throughout dinner as if trying to divine what had happened to the man. He appeared unconcerned, but Emaline knew something was up. He hadn't been interested in anything except work for months.

Speculatively she glanced at Ginny and then Joey, then back to her nephew.

Immediately following their evening meal, Mitch left for the office, with strict instructions for everyone to get to bed early, they would leave promptly at 4:30 in the morning.

Since Joey would be put in a hospital gown once they arrived, Ginny let him wear his pajamas the next morning for the ride in to the city. The air was crisp and cool, the stars still brilliant in the sky, dawn more than an hour away as they pulled away from the house. Ginny felt keyed up, a bit apprehensive, and still amazed the operation was actually going to take place. Even when she paid Mitch back the money, she'd never be able to repay his kindness to a stranger.

Mitch drove swiftly through the dark, saying little, listening to his aunt. Emaline sat in the front with him, sipping coffee Rosita had prepared, and chatting almost nonstop. Ginny tried to relax, but she was edgy and nervous. Her precious little boy was having surgery!

All thanks to the man driving. A complex creature whom she would never have suspected of warmth from their first encounter. Yet who was singlehandedly doing more for her son than anyone else ever had. Once again she wished he had been Joey's father. Not that Mitch would have acted like Joey's father had, but a woman could dream.

Once they arrived at the hospital, he handled everything efficiently and with no wasted energy. Before Ginny realized it, Joey had been wheeled away and she was left in the surgery waiting room with Mitch and Emaline—with four hours ahead before Joey could be seen again.

Restless, she paced the small waiting room, praying Joey's good spirits would hold, that the operation would be a success, that nothing would go wrong.

"Let's go for breakfast," Mitch suggested, glancing around. "This place makes me edgy."

"I couldn't eat anything," Ginny replied.

"I could. And you need to. He'll be raring to go when he's out of here—you are already too thin. You need to put some pounds on," Mitch said.

"He's right, dear. We will need all our energy

when he's home. I think a nice breakfast will help in more ways than one. We can't just keep our eye on the clock, time would pass too slowly,'' Emaline said, adding her weight to the argument.

Outnumbered, Ginny nodded. "But only as far as the hospital cafeteria. I'll leave word at the nurses' station."

While the cafeteria was not crowded—it was too early—there were still several people ordering ahead of them. Ginny decided to have an omelet made to order. Emaline wandered to the cereal display. Mitch came up behind Ginny watching the short-order cook as he scrambled eggs, fried them and kept a steady stream of bacon and sausages cooking.

"Why did you change your mind and decide to come today?" she asked, glancing up at him. "Was it something Gloria said?"

"No, I had decided before seeing her. I began thinking yesterday on the ride back to the house what I would want someone to do for Marlisse had the circumstances been different. I don't know who used my name five years ago, but it tied us together.'' He hesitated a moment, as if gearing up for a difficult confession, then continued, "I'll never get to see my daughter grow up, get married, provide me with grandchildren. But I used to like kids. Still do, I guess. I've shut myself away from them lately. Marlisse and Daisy both would be disappointed. Maybe helping Joey can show them I haven't abdicated life's responsibilities just because they are no longer here with me."

"You're a kind man, Mitch. Anyone else would have shut the door in my face or cried fraud or something that first afternoon,'' Ginny said. She hated feeling so beholden, but would do almost anything for her son. She just hoped at some point in her life, she could pass on the kindness.

He glanced around then leaned close, almost whispering in her ear. ''I have a reputation in this town, don't you dare repeat you think I'm kind!''

Ginny laughed, as she suspected was his intent. His dark eyes gazed down into hers. For a moment she longed to step into his arms, rest in the safety they offered. She yearned to feel his mouth on hers again, to lean against his strength. She wished she had that right with an intensity that frightened her.

But, as Aunt Edith always said, that which doesn't harm us makes us stronger. Ginny had been on her own for years, nothing had changed since meeting Mitch. She deliberately stepped away from temptation.

She had to be strong for her son. There was only the two of them against the world. This time with Mitch was magical—but fleeting. Soon they'd be on their way back to Florida, with memories to last a lifetime. And a debt she could never fully repay.

Less than an hour passed before they returned to the surgery waiting room. Mitch hesitated in the doorway, then looked at Ginny. ''Emaline will stay with you. I can't stay here. I'm going into work.'' He pulled a cell phone from his pocket. ''Press here and here,'' he showed her, ''and it will ring directly to my office. Let me know as soon as you hear something.''

''Okay.'' Ginny took the phone, disappointed he

wasn't staying, but trying not to show it. He'd already given her more time than she had a right to expect.

Once he left, she let down her guard.

"I expect it was hard for him to be here, don't you think?" she asked Emaline, feeling the anxiety creep in. She prayed her son would be all right.

"He had to go to the hospital when he was called about Marlisse and Daisy—to identify them. I don't expect any experience with such a facility will ever be easy in the future. It will always hold memories of that horrible day," Emaline said.

Ginny nodded. It made his coming and staying as long as he did even more special. She just couldn't help wishing he'd stayed a little longer.

The rest of the morning seemed to drag by in a blur. She and Emaline talked desultorily. She leafed through magazines, paced to the window and tried not to watch the clock.

Finally the surgeon came out to report on the success of the operation. Ginny was allowed in to the children's recovery room to await Joey's return to consciousness. He had bandages over his left eye, and looked so small and pale in the big bed her heart turned over.

She dialed Mitch.

He answered at the first ring.

"Hi, it's me. Joey's out of surgery. Every thing went well." Ginny burst into tears.

"Ginny?"

She tried to stop the tears, but the relief was so overwhelming, she couldn't.

"Tell me!" he ordered.

"Everything is fine," she repeated, trying to speak

coherently. What a ninny. She should have waited to call him, or at least waited to fall apart.

"I'll be right there."

He disconnected before she could protest.

A nurse stopped in, saw Ginny and came to check on her, rubbing her shoulder compassionately when she learned of the reason for the tears.

"It's hard when they are kids, isn't it?" she said, offering a tissue. "But he's going to be fine, and better than before. Dr. Tamsin has a well-deserved reputation for doing outstanding work. Joey won't wake up for a while, and when he finally does, he'll be groggy and ready to go back to sleep almost immediately. You have time to go for a cup of tea if you like."

Ginny shook her head. "I'll wait here. Sorry to be a bother."

"No bother, he's a lucky boy to have a doting mother." The nurse patted her on the shoulder again, checked Joey's vital signs and moved on to the second occupied bed in the recovery room.

Ginny bunched up the tissue and watched her son sleep. He was going to be fine, his eyes fixed and able to track like everyone else. She was so relieved the ordeal was over.

Ten minutes later Mitch strode into the Recovery Room, heading straight for Ginny. She looked up, surprised.

"Mitch, what are you doing here?"

He leaned over her. "Are you all right? Is Joey all right?"

She nodded, feeling the tears well in her eyes.

"I came as soon as I could. Traffic was a bear."

He studied her for a moment, then looked at Joey. "If he's going to be okay, why the tears? Was there a complication after all?"

"No, it was just the relief," she said, trying to staunch the new flow of tears with the bunched up tissue. Mitch had left work to come because he thought she needed him. The knowledge overwhelmed her. No one had ever done that for her before. Tears were the only way to relieve the tension that filled her.

"Here," he thrust a clean handkerchief into her hand. As she blotted her eyes, he pulled her to her feet and wrapped his arms around her. Ginny had never felt so safe. She leaned slightly against him, relishing his arms holding her, the steady comforting beat of his heart beneath her ear, the feeling that life would go on and she would make it.

All from being held in his embrace.

How lucky Marlisse had been to have such a wonderful man for her husband. For long moments, she drew strength from him. Then Ginny drew a shaky breath and stepped back, breaking his hold. She couldn't allow her boss to hold her. It wasn't right.

Not only that, she was enjoying it too much. She needed to keep some distance between them. He had done so much for them, she didn't want him to think she expected anything further.

She had to remind herself she worked for him. Temporarily. When Helen returned, Ginny would be on her way back to Florida before she could say order-up.

The thought was depressing, but she clung to it and put some distance between them.

"Thank you for coming. I really am a silly goose to be so teary when the news is good. But it's such a relief!" she said.

Mitch gestured to the chair and Ginny sat. He perched on the arm and asked what she'd been told about Joey's recovery.

When learning that once Joey recovered from the anesthetic he would still be groggy and tired and most likely go right back to sleep, Mitch insisted she go to the hotel later to get a good night's rest.

"I wanted to stay here."

"He'll be asleep, Ginny. He won't even know if you are here or not. We'll be less than five minutes away and can come in an instant if there is a need. But if he sleeps through the night, it will give you time to sleep as well. You'll want to be rested for tomorrow."

She studied her son as Mitch studied her. She looked tired, and it was still early afternoon. She needed rest to keep her energy up. And to eat more. Had she and Emaline had lunch?

He rose, intent on finding his aunt and making sure she took care of Ginny.

She drew her gaze from Joey to look at him. "Are you leaving?"

"Do you want me to stay?"

Hesitating, she shook her head. "No, I'm fine. There's nothing you can do."

He knew that. But for an instant he wished there was something he could do to help. To shelter her from the trials and tribulations of life. He didn't want to analyze that protective streak too closely.

The thought shocked him. He didn't normally go

into some protective mode. Ginny had lived her entire life until a couple of weeks ago without his help. She'd do fine without it in the future.

He was growing too involved with her and her son. Losing Marlisse and Daisy had been almost more than one man could stand. He refused to put his emotions on the line a second time. Getting involved with women, and especially children, was risky. Getting involved with this particular woman was not in the cards. She'd come looking for someone else. She was still searching for the man she'd loved enough to make a child with. He wasn't that man.

And he couldn't offer any woman what she'd want—a devoted husband, father to her children, a future. The risk of further heartache was too great. Once in a lifetime was all he could endure.

"I'll look up Aunt Emaline and return to work. Call me if you need me."

She nodded, and tried to smile. "Thanks for coming over. Sorry to interrupt whatever you were doing."

Ginny watched as Mitch left the large recovery room. He looked so fit and robust striding across the floor, one of the nurses stepping out of his way and then turning to watch. He looked neither to the right or left. Probably couldn't wait to get out of the hospital.

But her heart warmed at the reality of his coming. He'd thought she needed him and he came at once.

Such a contrast to the man she'd thought she'd loved so many years ago. He had vanished without a trace—after leaving a string of lies. She had been gullible, as Aunt Edith had said. She was wiser now. And almost regretted the fact.

Mitch would never lie. A woman would know exactly where she stood with him. As Ginny did. He had helped Joey because he could no longer help his own daughter. But there was no tie beyond that—no matter how much she might wish there were.

Emaline insisted Ginny take breaks from sitting by the bed of the sleeping child. When they moved Joey to the Pediatrics Floor, Ginny went for a quick walk around the hospital grounds. The fresh air felt good, but it was a short break, she wanted to be at his side when Joey awoke.

It was after seven when Ginny agreed to leave with Emaline. Joey had been awake, eaten a light meal and drifted back to sleep. The nurse on duty had told Ginny she expected Joey to sleep all night. The drip from the IV would keep him hydrated, nourished and pain free, so there was no reason for him to waken before morning.

Agreeing to call if he did, she shooed Ginny and Emaline away from his bed.

They took a cab to the hotel, Ginny feeling wrung out and cranky.

"We'll order room service, I think," Emaline said as they rode up in the elevator. "A quick shower will revive you long enough to eat. I know you're tired, but you need to eat, as well as sleep. Actually once we finish dinner it'll be bed for both of us. I'm not used to getting up so early and then spending the day away from home. I didn't even get a chance to nap!"

"Oh, Emaline, you shouldn't have stayed all day," Ginny said, feeling guilty.

The elevator stopped on their floor and the elderly lady headed for their suite. "Nonsense. I love that boy, too, you know. I had to be near in case. Rosita and I are looking forward to taking care of him while he recovers. No strenuous exercise for six weeks, the doctor said. We've got cards and board games and videos lined up. She asked her grandchildren what they liked the best, so we have exactly what will appeal to a boy that age. But it's a surprise, something new for each day, so don't be telling him anything!"

"He'll love it. Thank you." Ginny gave her an impulsive hug. Where would she be without these people helping her? It was so unexpected she still felt she was dreaming.

Mitch was on the phone in the sitting room of the suite when they entered. He quickly ended the call and rose to greet Emaline and Ginny. He studied Ginny closely, then seemed satisfied.

"Did you two eat?" he asked.

"We wanted room service," Emaline said. "Did you eat?"

"No, I called the hospital just as you two were leaving, so I waited."

The service was quick and before long the three of them shared a meal in front of the large window that overlooked Dallas. The lights shining from the buildings and dwellings coupled with the streetlights gave a fairytale glow to the land. When she had finished dinner, Emaline excused herself and headed for bed.

"Are you too tired to stay up a little longer?" Mitch asked Ginny.

"No, I'm still keyed up from today's events. I still can't believe the operation I've saved for so long is over. Of course this only means the beginning of more treatment and therapy, but according to the doctor within a few months, both eyes will track together. We owe it all to you."

"You would have managed, just taken a little longer," he murmured.

"I wish I could repay you, beyond the money, I mean. You don't know how grateful I am."

"I'm not after gratitude," he growled.

Ginny fell silent. What was he after? As far as she could tell, Mitch went through the motions of living, but a part of him had died with Marlisse and Daisy.

She understood it. She had thought life had ended when her John Mitchell Holden had disappeared. But she'd had a baby to care for, and gradually life had regained its glow. Until Aunt Edith had died. One of the hardest aspects of death was the fact those surviving had to move on. Life continued. And it never came with any guarantees it wouldn't try to crush you beneath its blows.

Ginny hadn't been crushed, though it seemed like it at the time. She wished she could do something to show him life still had much to offer.

Mitch stared at Ginny. He saw color rise in her cheeks, and her eyes dart toward his, then away, as if afraid to meet his gaze lest she see something in it she didn't want to see.

And that would be what, he thought heavily. Lust? When she said she was grateful, anger flared. He didn't want that. He wanted something more. He'd kissed her, tasted the sweetness of her mouth. And he wanted more.

For the first time in years, his libido sprang to life at the thought of someone beside Marlisse. He wanted Ginny Morgan.

Emotions churning, he pushed back his chair and walked to the window. Leaning against the sill with both hands, he stared sightlessly out into the dark. The lights twinkling gave no delight. He was looking inward and hated what he saw.

Desire for a woman beside his wife. It didn't matter that Marlisse had been dead for two years. It felt like betrayal. Betrayal of her, of his vow to remain uninvolved. Betrayal of the trust Ginny had placed in him. Damn, he could control it. He would. Taking a deep breath, he almost jumped when she touched his arm. He hadn't heard her move to cross the room.

Slowly he straightened and turned toward her. The lighting seemed bright after the darkness of the night. He narrowed his gaze against it, taking in the uncertainty of her expression, the soft swell of her breasts, the fragrance that whispered Ginny, Ginny, Ginny.

Without thinking, he drew her into his arms and lowered his head. The first touch of her lips drove all thoughts from his mind. Guilt fled. Desire sparked. This felt too right to be wrong.

Marlisse was gone. Ginny was here. Alive, warm, sweet and so sexy it drove him crazy!

She held nothing back as he deepened the kiss. His tongue touched hers, mated, swept through her mouth as if he would devour her. Heat rose between them, and he could feel her breasts press against his chest, feel them swell with desire. Her arms were wound around his neck and she held on as if she'd never let him go.

One kiss would never be enough. He wanted her as a man wants a woman, completely, totally. He rubbed his hands down her back, lifting her closer, nestling against her as if he'd sought comfort, or more.

Every breath was filled with her scent. Every heartbeat increased his body heat until he felt he would ignite. His mouth against hers only had him longing to touch other parts of her. He moved to kiss her cheeks, trail short nibbles along her jaw, down to the rapidly beating pulse point at the base of her throat. When he licked it, her skin was pure ambrosia. She moaned softly in her throat and he felt as if he could capture the sound with his lips.

He brushed back the collar of her blouse and tasted the softness of her shoulders. He felt her own mouth move against his ear, along his cheek, back to his lips.

Mindful of Aunt Emaline only a few steps away, he knew they couldn't go anywhere with this—even if Ginny would agree.

Slowly reality returned. He kissed her mouth gently one last time and eased her away, gazing down into her slightly blurred eyes.

She blinked slowly and met his gaze confusion and desire mingled.

''If that was because you're grateful, I'll put my fist through the wall,'' he murmured.

She shook her head. ''I might be grateful, but for that I'd just say thank you.'' She reached out and trailed her fingers down his cheek, rubbed against the evening beard along his jaw as if mesmerized by the texture, by the slight rasping sound. Her eyes followed her fingertips for a moment, then met his gaze once again.

"Why did you kiss me?" she asked softly.

"Because I want you."

At her startled look, he almost smiled. She had to have known from the level of the kiss there was more than just a brush of lips.

"Been there, done that. It sure didn't turn out the way I thought it would," she said flippantly. She was flat-out scared. She'd thought she had love the man she knew as John Mitchell, but it had proved false. She didn't trust her senses, her own mind or heart. She could fall for this man, and end up the same way—alone with a boatload of regrets.

Backing away, she looked so sad Mitch wanted to grab her up in another embrace and kiss her until she couldn't think of anything or anyone else. Make her forget the past.

But she was obviously remembering another time. Another man. Could he blame her for being wary? Especially when all he wanted was time with her, a few hours, days. Not a future, not forever.

"Go to bed, Ginny. Tomorrow you'll have your hands full with Joey."

A weaker man would have been hurt by the swiftness of her departure, he thought cynically. But he suspected she was the wiser of the two of them.

CHAPTER SEVEN

A WEEK later Ginny had almost forgotten the kiss. At least that was what she told herself endless times during the day whenever the memory of that night arose.

The first few days Joey was home from the hospital were hectic. Mindful of her obligation, she took an hour or two each day to check the mail. The office phone was switched to ring in the house and she took messages from there. Mitch spent the week in Dallas, not even returning home in the evenings.

She wondered if he deliberately stayed away, but found it unlikely. He did what he wanted and wouldn't be embarrassed by her flight that night. She was the one who wished she'd handled things differently, more sophisticatedly.

She had been a wildly willing participant in that kiss. Why wouldn't he think she'd be opened to more? Especially in light of what he knew of her history.

But she'd been hurt too much by the defection of Joey's father. She was a coward—afraid to risk her heart again. Especially with a man who had buried his own heart with his wife and child.

Ginny finally put in a full day in the office, filing letters and reports, answering the phone, receiving faxes from Mitch's far-flung empire. She was growing adept at office work and liked it. Maybe she'd try for a desk job when she returned to Florida instead of working at the Shrimp Shack.

Just before four she heard a familiar engine in the driveway. She rose and hurried to the window in anticipation. Mitch had returned. Ginny watched as he walked into the house, with not even a glance in the direction of the office.

She sighed softly, knowing her decision to flee the other night had been wise, but wishing things were different. Wishing she could make Mitch remember what it was to embrace life to the fullest, to enjoy the companionship of another, to plan for a future together. To love.

She blinked, and drew in a sharp breath.

She was not in love with her boss!

Delaying as long as she could, Ginny stretched out her final tasks, not wanting to appear anxious to see Mitch, just because she hadn't seen him in days. She had spoken briefly to him on the phone—it wasn't enough.

Finally at close to five, she shut off the computer, turned on the answering machine and headed for the house. She'd check on Joey, change for dinner and try to contain her impatience until she saw Mitch again.

It wasn't necessary. As soon as she approached Joey's room, she could hear the deep rumble of Mitch's voice.

"So how come you don't have a little girl anymore," Joey asked.

Ginny quickened her step. She hoped Mitch wouldn't blast her son with some scathing answer. Joey was just a little boy.

She couldn't hear the words, but the tone was soft, quiet. Pausing at the doorway, she surveyed the scene before her. Emaline was sitting in the rocker next to Joey's bed. Mitch was perched on the edge, with what looked like an entire arm of action heroes spread out on the bed around Joey.

"…accident."

"Wasn't she wearing her seat belt?" Joey asked, his one visible eye wide as he stared at Mitch.

"Yes, both she and her mother were wearing their seat belts. But the crash was too severe. It wasn't enough to save them."

Emaline had tears in her eyes. Ginny swallowed, wondering how they had arrived at this conversation. She ached for the sorrow in Mitch's voice, for the tears Emaline shed, and for the tragic loss of young life.

"Maybe I could be your new little boy. Then you wouldn't be so lonely," Joey said.

"Joey!" Ginny stepped inside. Time to nip that kind of thinking in the bud.

"Hi Mommy. Did you know Mitch had a little girl but she died?"

"I did know. It's sad, isn't it?"

Mitch rose and turned.

She nodded in greeting. "I didn't know to expect you back today."

"Change of plans. I have to go to L.A. tomorrow. I want you to come with me." He gave no hint of the passion they'd shared, of the heat and excitement of his kiss. He was her boss merely reacting to business needs.

"Go with you? I can't. I have Joey—"

"Whom Emaline and Rosita dote on and care for as if he were their own. No harm will come to the boy."

"For how long we would be gone? I've never really been away from Joey." She looked at her son, her heart swelling in love. The bandages were due to be removed next week. The prognosis was outstanding. She knew Emaline and Rosita loved watching him, but still, it was a lot to ask of a mother who had never spent the night away from him before his hospital stay.

"A couple of days at most. He'll be fine."

"Now dear, don't worry about Joey. We'll watch him like he was our own," Emaline said, rising and brushing down the flowing skirt of her soft peach dress. Her white hair was neat even after a day of watching a mischievous four-year-old. She smiled at Joey. "We'll have fun while your mom is away, won't we?"

"Where are you going?" A hint of panic touched her son voice.

"On a business trip to Los Angeles," Mitch said, his gaze never leaving Ginny. "I'll tell you what, Joey. If you're good, I'll have Tom bring in one of the dogs so you can see him while we're gone?"

"Every day?"

Ginny hid a smile, and felt a small pang. Her son was not above negotiating. She wasn't sure how to feel knowing a dog would make up for her being gone.

"Every day."

"Okay. Bring me back a present," he loftily commanded his mother.

"We'll see. Nothing's been decided," she said.

"I know it's short notice. Helen always keeps a suitcase packed for just such sudden trips. Can you be ready by morning?" Mitch asked.

Ginny shook her head. "I don't have any clothes that would be appropriate. All I brought were jeans and shorts—and only enough for a few days. I had no idea at the time I'd be here so long."

It seemed another lifetime that she'd arrived and been so disappointed not to find Joey's father. Now she had a difficult time even remembering what he looked like or what appeal he'd had for her five years ago.

"You can pick up some things once we get there. I had us booked on the nine a.m. flight. We have reservations for a suite at the Innsbrook on Wiltshire Boulevard. With any luck, we'll be done in two days and home that night."

Ginny had a hard time concentrating on anything after the word suite. It conjured up memories of the last suite they shared—with Emaline. Only this time it would be only the two of them. When she realized Mitch and Emaline were both looking at her oddly, she nodded. "Fine. I'll be ready first thing tomorrow."

Afraid to give away her thoughts, she turned to head for her room with a murmured "see you in a bit" for Joey.

Mitch stopped her before she reached the door. "Ginny?"

She stopped, turned. He came closer until she breathed in the scent of his aftershave mingled with the masculine scent that was Mitch's own. Heat from his body enveloped her and she tried desperately to remember he was her boss, nothing more.

"You are not worried about traveling with me, are you?" he asked.

"Should I be?" Her heart was pounding, she hoped he could not tell. Feeling much as a schoolgirl with a first crush, she tried to compose her thoughts and her features to hide any indication. How embarrassing for both of them if Mitch ever suspected how she felt about him.

"No. I had Jasmine reserve a suite for convenience. You'll have your privacy and I'll have mine. But if I need work done late at night, then it would be better for both of us to be readily available."

"I understand." She waited a moment, but he said nothing further.

"I'll see you at dinner," she said and escaped into the bedroom. Leaning against the door, she rested her head on the wooden panels. He'd have his room and she'd have hers, but they'd still be close. As close as they were in this house but with no else around who knew them. Maybe she should make up an excuse and stay here.

But the thought of traveling with Mitch, of seeing him in action was too tantalizing. It wouldn't be long now before Helen would be back. Then Ginny's time in Texas would be up and she and Joey would have to head back to Florida. Surely she could handle a few days in Los Angeles.

Mitch stared at the closed door feeling like an idiot. He didn't have to explain why he'd booked a suite. Once there she would have seen the obvious advantages for working together. Not that he and Helen shared a suite when they traveled. But they had worked together for many years, so fell into a pattern.

Ginny was new to office work. She might have a question or something.

Yeah, right, he scoffed as he headed back downstairs and out to the office.

Truth be told, he didn't really need Ginny to accompany him. He could have made do with the clerical staff in the L.A. office. But he wanted her to go. Wanted to, what, show her off?

He stopped inside the office staring at her desk, struck by the idea. Show her off? To whom? People who worked for him? Friends?

And to what purpose? Helen would be back soon, and Ginny's reason for being in Texas would vanish. How soon would she pack and leave?

Frowning at the mere idea, Mitch continued into his office and reached for the messages piled up at his desk.

Ginny had never flown before, so she had nothing to compare with their flight to the coast. But the wide, comfortable seats, and the lovely place setting of linen napkins and heavy silverware delighted her senses. Of course Mitch only traveled first-class. She felt woefully underdressed in her faded jeans and yellow top. Most of the passengers in first class were obviously businessmen and women wearing dress-for-success suits and carrying laptops and leather briefcases.

She should have refused to travel, she thought as she slid down in her seat, glad she was by the window. Gazing out the small opening, she tried to imagine herself somewhere else. She hoped no one was looking at her wondering what she was doing on board.

"You're not feeling sick are you?" Mitch asked.

She shook her head, her gaze fixed on the men loading baggage into the plane.

"Did you bring something to read?" he asked as the flight attendant began walking through the cabin offering magazines.

She shook her head.

"What did you expect to do on the flight?"

She looked at Mitch. "I don't know. What do you usually do."

"Work."

"You work all the time."

"It gets me through the day," he said.

"So tell me what's so important about the Los Angeles situation you have to go there in person," she invited.

Mitch hesitated only a moment, then as if assured of her interest, began to explain the personnel and production crisis that he wanted to directly change. Soon he began explaining the entire operation to her.

Ginny was fascinated. She had picked up bits and pieces as she'd worked for him, but to have him explain the connections and the relationship of the people she'd spoken with, it became clear he ran a complex business consortium, and ran it well.

"And the ranch, that's such a small part of it."

"It's been my family's home for several generations, but I never wanted to be a full-time rancher. I like participating in the branding, the roundup, and

directing how we are going to rotate fields, which bull
to try next, but my heart isn't in it completely. Not
like my father's was.''

"That's so sad.''

"What is?''

"To think it's been in your family for so long and
after you, there's no one.''

He looked startled, then pensive. "Not in the direct
line, but I have cousins. My grandparents are their
grandparents and great-grandparents who owned the
land, too. They're family.''

She nodded in agreement, afraid she'd spoken out
of turn. The love he had for his home shone through
when he spoke of it. It might rival his love for business, but nothing would dislodge it. How sad to have
no children to leave the legacy to. No one to share in
love of the land that had been part of their family for
generations.

They were more than halfway to L.A. when he
turned the tables and asked her about her life in
Florida.

Ginny wasn't sure how much he really wanted to
know, so glossed over many things, telling him about
working at the Shrimp Shack, and about Joey's love
for the ocean.

"Your friend Maggie's name comes up frequently,
when you talk,'' Mitch commented at one point. "But
no man's. Do you have a special male friend? Or are
you still waiting for Joey's father?''

Ginny shook her head. "No time nor inclination
for men—new or old.''

"Why not? You're young and pretty. I'd think the

young men in Ft. Lauderdale would be flocking around.''

''I've never had a flock,'' she replied quietly. ''And dating a single mother isn't as glamorous as dating a swinging single with no attachments.''

''Their loss.''

She smiled, warmed by the comment. For several seconds her eyes locked with his. In another time, another place would they have found they had anything in common? Would the attraction she felt flare whenever he was around grow into something shared by both of them? Should she even mention she no longer thought of Joey's father except to let him know he had a son? Why would Mitch care.

Wishful thinking. She'd tried happy-ever-after with the man she had once known as John Mitchell Holden. He was nothing like the real thing. She didn't know who he had been, or where he was now, but she was grateful she'd had the chance to meet Mitch.

''We'll go shopping when we reach L.A. Rodeo Drive has some nice stores.''

''Rodeo Drive!'' Even she had heard of the ritzy, trendy thoroughfare renowned through the world for expensive luxuries. ''I think a more traditional department store would suit better,'' she said.

''Since the need for clothes are business related, the company will pick up the tab,'' Mitch said casually.

''I can't let you buy my clothes! You've already done so much with Joey—''

''Don't argue, Ginny. It's a business related expense, all right? You wouldn't need anything if you weren't helping me with the work here. I don't care to discuss the matter any more.''

Several hours later when they finally checked into the Innsbrook Hotel, Ginny was tired, hungry and secretly elated with the selections she'd chosen. The suit would be perfect for job interviews if she decided to follow through when she returned to Florida. There were three separate tops to wear with it, two in cream and one in flaming red!

And the dress Mitch had insisted she needed for the dinner meeting planned was daring and darling. She had never owned anything so glamorous, yet the salesclerk continued to call it a subdued little black dress that would go from work to date with a few accessories, which she then sold as a package complete with shoes.

''I'll order a snack for us from room service while you change,'' Mitch said when they entered the lavish suite. ''As soon as we're done, we'll head for the office—before the traffic gets any worse.''

''The traffic could get worse?''

''When it's rush hour, they open the shoulders as another lane and it's still backed up for miles in every direction. Wear the suit, tomorrow we'll be having dinner with the Morrises and the Turners. We'll probably just work through dinner tonight, order something at the office.''

Ginny took her time dressing, wanting to make sure she looked the part of competent personal assistant to Mitch Holden. When she stepped from her room into the sitting area, she felt more sophisticated than ever before.

Mitch frowned when he looked at her.

"Doesn't it suit me?" she asked.

"You look remote, older. Not like at home."

"I'm your efficient, competent secretary. How will people respect that if I look like a kid wearing jeans?" she countered.

Amusement lit his eyes. "Efficient and competent, huh?"

She flushed. "Well, I want to look the part at least."

"You've done well, especially for someone without a secretarial background. Come have something to eat. I want to leave soon."

The rest of the day passed in a whirl. Ginny met the key players at the Los Angeles office. While there was some brief comments made about Helen's absence, she had already talked to most of the staff on the phone, so they had known to expect her. She didn't try to do more than she knew how. The others respected her for it, and were more than helpful.

Mitch was in his element. She watched fascinated as he took control, without blatantly stepping on toes. There was no question the other men respected his business savvy and took their direction from him.

When they began to talk about multimillion dollar mistakes, her eyes widened. Focusing on the notebook and notes she was taking for Mitch, she tried to adjust her thinking. The man was far wealthier than she'd suspected if this was merely one portion of the many companies he directed. No wonder funding Joey's operation hadn't been a hardship for him.

She still planned to repay him, but more from her own sense of honor than any need for money on his part.

Ginny fell asleep immediately after her head hit the pillow later that night. The day had started early in Texas and ended late in California. Did he keep up such a hectic pace normally?

She gave no thought to Mitch only a room away. Grateful for the break, she slept through the night without interruption.

Mitch checked his watch once again. It was after seven and he had not heard a single sound from Ginny's room. Their breakfast would be arriving soon.

He walked to the window and drew open the drapes. L.A. was on the move, cars and buses crowding the streets, the high morning fog from the sea mere wisps of gray against at pale blue sky.

He walked to her door and listened. Nothing. Knocking softly, he waited. Had she wakened earlier and gone out for a walk?

Mitch turned the knob and pushed the door open slightly, peering into Ginny's room. She was still fast asleep, on her side, her face resting on one hand like a child.

Stepping in, he watched her sleep for several seconds. She looked younger, more like the Ginny he'd come to know over the last few weeks than the woman who had worn the trappings of corporate employee yesterday.

That had startled him. He never noticed what Helen wore. She was always suitably turned out for whatever meeting or social event they attended. Yet on Ginny, it had looked artificial.

He liked the way she normally looked, he realized.

Like now, her skin flushed from sleep, her hair in disarray around her head. The soft rise and fall of her breasts as she slept drew his eyes.

Desire hit him like a powerful punch. He wanted her as he hadn't wanted anyone in a long time. Maybe ever. She was a pretty woman, but not beautiful. She seemed so innocent despite having a child and making her living on her own for several years. Maybe it was because of the hardships she'd survived that he admired her so much.

Or because of her cheerful attitude despite difficulties that would overwhelm another person.

He liked having her in his life, he realized. Even Joey was growing on him, despite his vow to remain apart from potentially hurtful situations.

"Ginny?" he called softly.

She didn't stir. Mitch noted it for future reference—Ginny slept deeply and wasn't easy to awaken.

"Ginny?" His voice a bit louder, he entered her room and crossed to the bed. Hesitating only a moment, he placed his hand on her shoulder registering instantly the warmth of her soft skin, the silky texture. Shaking her gently, he left his hand there, absorbing the feel of her against his palm.

"Ginny, it's time to get up. We have a lot to do today."

Her eyes came open slowly. For a moment he recognized her confusion. Then she met his gaze and looked startled. Reluctantly Mitch removed his hand, wishing he could come up with a reason not to.

"How late is it?" She sat up. Suddenly aware of the barely-there nightie she wore, she pulled the sheet up to her chin.

"It's after seven. Breakfast will be here any minute and I want to leave by eight."

"I'll be ready!"

Mitch strode from the room without a backward glance. He dare not risk further perusal of his lovely temporary secretary. The wispy nightie had surprised him, though if he thought about it he couldn't say exactly why. Probably since she normally wore jeans and cotton shirts, he had expected her nightwear to be plain and practical.

She constantly surprised him. He had expected her to make a play for him, but she remained aloof, unless he counted the kisses they'd shared. There had been nothing aloof about her response.

Was she playing a deep game, or was she inexperienced?

Not totally, of course, she had a son after all. But there was an innocence around her that contrasted to her tough I-can-do-it-myself act. She had done well helping him out. She was devoted to her son.

And she fit in with Emaline. Even his own cousins had difficulty dealing with their aunt sometimes. But Ginny and Joey loved being in her company.

Mitch crossed to the window and gazed out over the L.A. landscape, mostly high-rises and freeways. He'd be glad to get back home, once the situation here was wrapped up. Would Ginny?

For a moment he toyed with the idea of offering Ginny a job that would keep her in Tumbleweed. She and Joey had friends in Florida, but no relatives. They could easily relocate to Texas. Joey would have a chance to grow up with horses and dogs, which all boys should be able to do.

She was touchy, however. He couldn't just make up something to hold her, it would have to be a legitimate job that didn't question her independence or smack of charity.

Room service delivered their breakfast just as Ginny emerged from her bedroom. They ate quickly and headed for the offices.

"Did you get all the notes from yesterday's meeting typed?" Mitch asked as their cab moved sluggishly through the rush-hour traffic.

"I did them on one of the computers and they were to be printed by Jason's secretary first thing so you'll have them once we arrive."

"Any problems?"

"None."

He glanced at her, noting how the suit skirt had ridden up a bit showing more of her tanned legs than he suspected she knew. Mitch grew uncomfortable, realizing that he wanted to reach out and run his fingertips along that smooth skin, feel the satiny softness, revel in the sweet texture he was sure to find.

Taking a deep breath, he looked out of the window on his side of the taxi, deliberately turning his thought to work and the muddle the L.A. office seemed to be in. But Ginny's scent tantalized, and her leaning forward from time to time to better see something had him constantly aware of her.

Maybe bringing her had been a mistake, but he'd wanted her with him. Not analyzing that closely, Mitch was relieved to see the office building come into view. Work was always the answer.

CHAPTER EIGHT

By six o'clock Ginny wanted to go back to the hotel, take a hot bath and go to sleep for twelve hours. Mitch was incredible. He knew more than she could ever remember, from employees' names and family situations, to the sales figures for the last several years, to the labor disputes and settlements that had been part of the company's history going back to its inception. She tried to keep up, but was lost more than half the time.

And what really annoyed her was Mitch looked as fresh and raring to go this late in the day as he had that morning. He had almost as much energy as Joey!

She slipped away from the round of farewells and placed a quick call to the ranch. It was two hours later there and she wanted to catch Joey before he went to bed. Chatting briefly with Emaline, she then spoke to her son. Reassured he was happy and well looked after, she reluctantly severed the connection sometime later. She missed him so much, but he was doing fine.

"Any problems?" Mitch joined her at the reception station. Closed for the day, Ginny had used that phone.

"None at all. Joey's been up and around. Emaline said they are keeping him from bending over, or doing too much, but he's glad to be out of bed. Are we ready to leave?"

"I told the Jim to let the Morrises know we meet them all at seven thirty at the Zorro's Mark. That give you enough time to change?"

She nodded, the dream of the hot bath fading. They'd dash back to the hotel, she'd change from the suit to that darling black dress, and then it would be back to business.

"Don't you ever get tired?" she grumbled as she picked up her purse and the file folder of notes and reports she was keeping for Mitch.

"Not often. Are you tired?"

She straightened up and headed for the elevators. "Not a bit," she fibbed. "But I don't keep up this pace all the time. I think I'd be exhausted if I did."

"I rest when I'm at the ranch."

She smiled at that. Some rest, riding the range, checking on the fencing, mustering cattle, not to mention fielding all the calls and faxes that routinely arrived. Still making decision that impacted every aspect of his myriad business interests.

"Something funny?"

Ginny shook her head. "I was just wondering what you call relaxing. What would you do at the beach, organize volleyball tournaments and swim meets?"

"I don't go to the beach often."

"Too restful, huh?"

"Too far."

"Don't you take some time off from time to time? Surely you took vacations with your family."

"When my wife and daughter were alive we went camping, and to theme parks. We even flew to the Calgary Stampede one year."

"But not the beach. Come visit us sometime, we'll see how long you can relax on the hot sand."

Ginny almost held her breath after the words were out. Would he suspect how much she wanted to keep in touch? How much she yearned for a relationship that would go beyond boss-secretary and maybe even develop into something lasting?

But Mitch didn't seem unduly suspicious about her comment, merely saying maybe. Which was a non-answer if she ever heard one.

When they arrived at the trendy restaurant later that evening, Ginny felt she was entering a dreamworld. The decor was lovely, expensive, with plenty of space around each table, not crowded together like the Shrimp Shack to accommodate as many diners at one time as possible.

There was even a dance floor at one end and a soft combo playing in the background.

When one of the men began to speak of work, Mitch raised an eyebrow. "Since we have our partners with us, who probably would be bored to tears with business discussions, let's keep the topics of general interest."

Ginny was surprised at his courtesy. She herself had thought it a business meeting. Soon she began to enjoy the evening—even more so when she and the others began to discuss Florida and the Atlanta beaches versus Southern California ones. That led to friendly banter about all the amenities in the two states.

Only when the talk veered to children did Ginny glance at Mitch, wondering if she should do something to deflect the conversation. She knew how much he ached for his own daughter. Would a discussion of soccer and dolls be too distressing?

He surprised her by relating an episode with Joey and the dogs at the ranch which had everyone chuckling. He didn't look devastated, didn't look as if he was going to leave the table if the conversation didn't change. She watched warily, and was startled when he gave her a wink. Blushing, she looked away. Mitch was fully capable of handling his own emotions, she admitted. If he didn't like the topic, he would change it!

When the meal was finished, Mitch ordered after dinner brandy and coffee for everyone. "Since the music is so appealing, I think it's time for some dancing."

"Oh, man, do you know how much I hate to dance?" Harry Morris groaned.

His wife laughed in delight. "Hey, I hear an order from the big boss man. Up and at 'em, Harry."

The man made a show of reluctance, but his grin let everyone there know he was teasing her.

When Jim and his wife rose, Mitch turned to Ginny. "Shall we?"

She could no more refuse him than she could refuse a request from Joey. To be held in his arms while they danced would be the best part of the evening. Feeling daring, she nodded. She would enjoy it as long as she didn't give herself away. She could not let Mitch know how much she liked being with him.

His hand on her back was warm, sending tendrils of awareness shivering through her. Pulling her close, he held her like a precious fragile object, one to be cherished. For a long moment, Ginny closed her eyes, savoring every aspect of being held in Mitch's arms.

The music was slow and dreamy. They moved in time with the rhythm, brushing thighs, pressing chest to breast, caught up in a world of two. Ginny felt as if she were on full alert, catching every nuance of the evening, from Mitch's heady scent, to the warmth of his hand against her back.

This is what life should be, she thought, two people who loved each other taking delight in being together. The quiet times alone were the best. She spared a brief moment of thought for Marlisse and Daisy. She'd never know them, but she could feel them in Mitch. Could he ever forget them and move on? Or not forget, but still make a new life—different, but just as good?

"I'm ready to head for the hotel," he said softly in her ear. "How about you?"

"If you want." Disappointment crashed down. He'd only done a duty dance. Now that it was finished, he wanted to leave. She'd been fooling herself for too long. Time for a reality check.

Mitch urged the others to stay. With a few last minute instructions to his colleagues, they said goodbye. In the morning Mitch and Ginny would return to Texas.

To Ginny's surprise, when they reached the hotel, Mitch stopped her as she headed for the elevator.

"They have a dance floor in the lower level bar of the hotel. Care to have a nightcap and dance a little longer?"

"I thought you were tired." Ginny couldn't hide

her surprise. Or the sudden surge of happiness that swept through her.

"Actually, I wanted to ditch the others and thought that excuse a diplomatic way to handle it—and hopefully not give rise to gossip."

"Why would there be gossip?"

"Anyone looking at us dancing together would immediately suspect we are something more than boss and secretary."

"They would?" Her heart kicked into high speed. "Why?"

"Because there is something more, and only a blind man would miss it. Dance?"

"Yes, please."

The dance floor in the hotel bar was almost empty, only two other couples took advantage of the hotel's ensemble. When Mitch swept her into his arms, Ginny knew she never wanted the night to end. Joey and her job and her life in Florida seemed to fade into the background. The evening had taken a surreal aspect, as if she were new and free and floating on gossamer wings. Mitch filled her senses, setting her aflame with what could be, what might be.

She loved Mitch Holding. It was different from anything she'd ever experienced—and much stronger and more mature than the feelings she had one thought she had for Joey's father.

She loved dancing with Mitch. Every brush of his body put hers on high alert. Every caress with his fingertips on the bare skin of her back had erotic images dancing in her mind, and cranked up the awareness another notch.

She loved talking with him, hearing his views on

issues, feeling the soft laughter when something stuck him funny—which was rare. He more often had a lurking sadness in his eyes. She cherished the amusement when she saw it, happy she could put it there.

She loved being with him, just to savor the moments, explore the scant time they had together before it all ended.

She felt like Cinderella at the ball, only there would be no magic glass slipper, no happy ever after ending. Her prince was not searching for a wife, but mourning one. And she didn't have a fairy tale godmother. One look at her situation would convince anyone of that.

But like Cinderella must have done at the ball, Ginny cherished every second. At least she have the memories to last all her days.

It was late when they finally moved to the elevators. Ginny felt wrapped in a time warp, almost afraid to say anything lest the mood be shattered and she had to face reality. A few more moments until she was in bed and she could relive each moment of the evening, imprinting it on her mind to remember forever.

"I had such a wonderful time," she said dreamily as the elevator doors closed. "I think I love L.A."

He pulled her against him in the empty elevator, his arm on her shoulder, his fingers rubbing light circles on her shoulder.

"Better than Tumbleweed?" he asked.

"Mmmm, maybe not. I like the ranch, Emaline, Rosita." She stopped before she said too much.

When they reached the suite, Mitch opened the door. The lights had been turned off, only the sparkling lights beyond the window illuminated the room.

"How pretty!" Ginny exclaimed at the sweep of lights as far as the eye could see.

"As pretty as you are," Mitch said, closing the door behind them and turning her in his arms.

When his mouth covered hers, Ginny gave herself up to his kiss. She yearned for him, craved his touch, longed for more. She had been lonely, but he filled the void and brought happiness. She had been alone, but with him felt as if two parts of a whole had come together.

Winding her arms around his neck, she opened her mouth when his tongue caressed her lips and danced with his when he swept in. She was glad for his strong arms as her bones seemed to soften and melt. If he wasn't holding them, she'd probably collapse on shaky knees.

Time spun away, there was only this moment, only the surging sensations that built and built. Ginny reveled in them, awed by the power of passion as it built, amazed at the desire that rose with each second. Oh if only it could last a lifetime!

"I want you, Ginny," he murmured, kissing her cheek, trailing nibbling kisses along her jaw, tilting back her head to lick and kiss down her neck to that rapid pulse point at the base of her throat. "Stay with me tonight."

Her heart leapt at his words. He wanted her as much as she wanted him! Had he gotten over his wife? Was he ready to move on—with her?

"I want you, too, Mitch," she said, burning with desire and longing. She tightened her own hold, drawing him closer.

He bent and lifted her into his arms, cradling her against his chest.

"I don't believe it!" she murmured, reaching up to kiss him along the jaw. "This only happens in movies."

He captured her lips with his as he walked easily into his bedroom. The lights from outside allowed him to see the shape and location of the bed. Gently settling her on the mattress, he slipped off her shoes, kneeling on the floor in front of her.

Ginny wished she could see him, see what his eyes said, see the expression on his face. Lacking sight, she relied on touch. His fingertips trailed up her leg, slipping beneath the skirt of the dress, trailing fire and ice in their wake. His voice was raspy when he spoke.

"No regrets, Ginny."

It felt like a dash of cold water. This wasn't her dream come true. It was one night out of time. A special night for just the two of them. But it was not a vow for the future, nor a promise she could hold on to.

"None," she replied, leaning over to frame his face in her palms and kissed him again. Feeling bold and daring she let him know how much she wanted him. For once she'd take what was offered and keep regrets at bay. She loved Mitch, could she deny herself a night in his arms?

When he surged up and pushed her gently back on the bed, she locked her arms around his neck and pulled him down with her.

Slowly they undressed each other, taking time to caress, kiss, touch. Any awkwardness with the process was ignored as passion rose and the surging need to become even closer drove them.

Just before Ginny fell asleep, the troubling thought arose. She hadn't confessed her love aloud, had she?

Daylight poured into the room when Mitch opened his eyes. An armful of delightfully warm female snuggled against him. Ginny's head was on his shoulder, one arm across his chest. Her legs were tangled with his. He could feel her breath on his bare chest.

His wife had been dead for two years. The first time he'd taken a woman out after Marlisse's death, he'd been consumed with guilt. The few dates he'd tried had been disasters. He had compared everyone to Marlisse.

Slowly he turned so he could see Ginny, hoping he didn't awaken her. He wanted a few moments alone. Her blond hair spilled across his arm, soft and silky as he'd always known it would be. She looked so young when she slept. All the worry and concerns of the day were smoothed away.

Surprised, he realized he wanted her again. He would awaken her with a kiss, caress that sexy little body until she was burning with the fire that had consumed them last night. She had been warm and loving and explosive. No guilt. No regrets.

He'd love to make love to her again, this time in the sunshine that was spilling into the room. He'd look into her eyes and see all the emotions she felt as they explored this new step.

And then what?

He shied away from thinking about the future. It

was enough to have her here in his bed, to be able to wake her with a kiss. To see where that would lead.

Slowly he drew her across his chest and kissed her awake.

No regrets, Mitch had said last night. But as Ginny stood in the shower sometime later, she had a boatload of regrets. She tried to tell herself she had not expected a declaration of undying devotion. That she had not expected the night together to change Mitch in any way. That she had not expected him to fall madly in love with her.

But she had lied to herself.

She wanted his love. She ached with her own love for him. Wished she was free to tell him, to touch him when she wished, to close the door when just the two of them were in a room and kiss him until he made love to her.

Instead, she was trying desperately to regain her equilibrium. Sighing softly, she closed her eyes, letting the warm water wash over her, caressing her skin as he had caressed her only a short time ago.

His touch had been so gentle, yet so arousing. Opening her eyes suddenly, she grabbed her washcloth and began to scrub. It was foolish to daydream for what couldn't be. Hadn't her aunt Edith said that over and over. A waste of time and energy.

Last night had been a magical evening out of time. But reality resumed. They had a flight to Dallas to catch, and before dinner would be back at the ranch. She had called a few moments ago and spoken with Joey. He was her primary concern. And her love for her son filled her heart. She would cherish her memories of Los Angeles, but move on as she had when she'd discovered Joey's father's perfidy.

How soon before Helen returned? Before she would never see Mitch Holden again? How would she bear walking away without a backward look. Face the future alone after knowing the delight of being with him?

Last night had shown her what she could have with a loving relationship with a man. And she wanted it with a fierce longing that almost scared her. Why couldn't he love her as she loved him? Yet how could she ever compete with a dead woman? The perfection of that relationship couldn't compare with her and the baggage of her past.

Ready at the designated time, Ginny wore her new suit, as if donning armor to aid in her defenses. She would not give into the need to touch him again. She was his temporary secretary, and would act the role. Determined to carry it off, she stepped into the sitting room.

Mitch stood near the window, studying the view. The famous Los Angeles smog had returned, the hazy air shimmering in the early morning heat. He turned when she entered, and Ginny was glad she'd dressed in her new role when she saw the remote expression on his face. She wasn't the only one to have regrets, despite their vow to have none.

"Ready?" he asked.

At her nod, he lifted the phone and called for a bellman, and requested a cab.

"I called Joey," she said as they waited awkwardly. Fiddling with the strap on her handbag, she glanced out the window, finding that easier than facing him. "He's fine. Says nothing hurts anymore and he wants to go riding."

"Once the doctor gives the go-ahead, we'll see about putting him up on a gentle mount."

She nodded, wondering if they'd still be at the ranch when the bandages came off. She mustn't forget their stay there was so temporary.

"Ginny—"

Mitch's statement was interrupted by a knock at the door. The bellman had arrived to take their luggage.

Any private conversation was impossible from then on. In no time they were dropped off at the curb at Los Angeles International Airport. Once they were through the security checks, Mitch suggested they get something to eat since their flight departure was still more than an hour away.

Ginny had no appetite, but since they hadn't eaten since dinner last night, she knew she had to give the appearance at least.

The trip home seemed endless. Ginny took two magazines on the plane with her and read them from cover to cover. Mitch seemed no more anxious to talk about last night than she did, engulfing himself in work, using the in-flight phone to touch base with the Dallas office and reaffirm some decisions made in Los Angeles.

Once in his car, she feigned sleep to avoid any conversation. She knew it was cowardice, but she couldn't help it. She needed to gain some distance before she could deal with the situation.

Of course she'd feel totally different if he gave the slightest indication last night had meant anything special to him. But his remote attitude drove her crazy and she refused to open the discussion for fear of what she might say or hear from him.

Once home, she almost ran to Joey's room. Hugging him when she dashed into the room, she felt her world stabilize. Here was her reality. Not some fairy tale dream come true with Mitch, but her precious son who needed her and whom she loved so much.

"I missed you, Mommy," Joey said.

"I missed you, too, sweetheart." She shrugged out of her suit jacket and tossed it over the end of the bed, perching beside Joey. "Tell me all you did."

"Hi, Mitch," Joey said.

Ginny looked at the man leaning casually against the doorjamb. Her heart caught as it normally did every time she saw him. She hadn't expected him to follow her.

"Hi Joey. How are you doing?"

"I'm almost all better. Aunt Emaline said if I had any more energy, they'd have to bottle it to sell." He almost bounced on the bed. "Rosita has games we played. Candyland is my favorite—only you don't get any real candy. And there's Chutes and Ladders. Her grandchildren play them and so I got to, too. And Aunt Emaline taught me how to play Go Fish. Can we play cards, Mommy? I'm really good. Aunt Emaline said I'm a natural."

Ginny nodded and laughed at his exuberance, all the while conscious of Mitch's brooding presence in the doorway. She flicked a glance at him from time to time, wondering what he was thinking. She hadn't expected him to stay through Joey's recitation. And his expression was anything but comfortable. But he didn't leave.

"Sounds like so much fun. We will have to get cards to take home with us," she said, wondering where she could also find the games. Maybe at a store in town. Otherwise she'd have to wait until they returned to Fort Lauderdale.

"I'm sure we have a few decks lying around. Joey can have a couple," Mitch said.

Ginny looked at him, struck by how lonely he looked—apart from them, standing in the doorway as if looking in on something he couldn't quite join. She longed to ask him to come sit on the bed, to tell Joey about their trip, but dare she? Did their night together give her anything more than memories? And if she did, what would he think? That she was trying to make more of their relationship than there was? Or did he just want to be included?

"Come in and tell Joey about card games you played as a child," she said, daring to try.

For a moment she thought he'd come in. But then he straightened. "I have work to do," he said, turning to leave.

Ginny's heart sank. She had hoped…

"Mommy, I got to see one of the dogs. Mr. Parlance brought him in. Rosita didn't like it, but Aunt Emaline said it was all right. He didn't have a tail but he wiggled all the time, and licked me!"

"I wish I had been here. Did you like the dog?" She tried to focus on Joey's animated descriptions of the working dog who had visited, but part of her followed Mitch. Had he gone to change? Would he head for the office? Or just close himself away in the study?

Already the trip to Los Angeles was fading.

Emaline waited for Ginny to begin dinner. Ginny still wore the skirt and blouse from the flight and was pleased Emaline liked it.

"Not as feminine and flowery as the dresses you like," Ginny said slipping into her place at the table.

"Ah, I do like my frilly dresses," Emaline said with a satisfied smile. "But they are not for everyone. That outfit suits you, and makes you look older, more mature. How did you fare in Los Angeles? It had been an age since I was there. If we had all gone, we could have taken Joey to an amusement park while Mitch worked."

"I went to help Mitch," Ginny reminded her gently. When Rosita entered carrying a platter of roast beef surrounded by new potatoes, Ginny smiled at her. "I hear I have you to thank for hours of fun Joey had playing board games."

"He is a delightful child. If he is here when my grandchildren come to visit, they will play well together."

"Why wouldn't he be?" Emaline asked. "And as soon as the bandages come off and they make sure his eye is repaired, he'll be rearing to go. Jack said he could help groom one of the gentler horses, if that is okay with you, Ginny. I don't see why not, Daisy had her own pony by this age, though she didn't take care of it all by herself. That would be too much for a child only four. But she could ride with a lead and loved to visit and talk with that pony. And feed it carrots. Remember, Rosita?''

''Indeed I do, Señorita. I will bring the rolls.''

Mitch's place had been set, but he had not arrived.

''Joey said you taught him how to play Go Fish,'' Ginny said as they began to eat.

''Daisy loved to play card games on a rainy day. She and Marlisse or she and Mitch or all three of them. Especially in the wintertime when Mitch didn't work outside, or have to go into Dallas. They would fix popcorn and spend the afternoon in front of the fire.'' The older woman grew pensive. ''I shall always miss them. They went far before their time.''

Ginny nodded, wondering if that was what Mitch had seen at the bedroom door—an echo of the times he and his wife played cards with their daughter. No wonder he hadn't wanted to come in and join them.

It was obvious he didn't plan to join them for dinner, either. Ginny tried to ignore the empty place, tried to focus on what Emaline was saying, but in her mind she remembered dinner last night, and the rest of the evening.

The next morning Ginny dressed in her usual jeans and pullover top. She had work to do. She could not dwell on fantasies that remained out of reach.

When she entered the office, she stopped in surprise. An immaculately groomed woman sat behind her desk. She looked up when Ginny entered.

''You must be Ginny Morgan.''

''And you're Helen.'' Ginny's heart dropped. There had been no warning from Mitch's assistant. She had returned as unexpectedly as she had left.

"Mitch rode out early this morning. I arrived just before he left," Helen said. She glanced around the desk. "You have done adequately in my absence. Of course he explained you weren't trained in secretarial work, which explains a lot."

Ginny flushed with embarrassment. She had done her best. Mitch had no complaints, once she mastered the fax machine. But she knew she'd never achieve all his paragon of a personal assistant had. And now Helen had returned.

"I hope things are all right here. And that your mother has recovered," Ginny said.

"The filing is up to date and the correspondence logged, I'll find my way around. My mother is recovering. Her sister is going to stay with her. So I have returned." It was a dismissal, loud and clear.

"I'll be at the house. Let me know if you can't find anything," Ginny said, turning around abruptly and retracing her steps head held high.

There was no reason to remain on the ranch, or in Texas beyond tomorrow when Joey had the bandages removed. Their doctor in Florida would be well able to take care of him over the next few months. Thanks to Mitch's generosity, Ginny still had some of her surgery fund which should cover medical follow-up expenses.

Of course there was the still matter of owing him for the operation, but she'd deal with that once she was back home and sure about a job. Maybe she could work out a repayment plan. It would only take two or three lifetimes at her wages. Still, something might turn up.

After Helen's comments however, she might reevaluate her desire for office work. Maybe she wasn't cut out for that after all.

She entered the house and went up to her room. The lilac room, not the rose room which might have made her look flushed. She smiled sadly, remembering Emaline's convoluted conversation that first day. She would miss her so much!

Drawing her suitcase from the back of the closet, she began to pack. She'd take care of Joey's clothes next and they could drive to Dallas in the morning, have the surgeon check him and then head for Florida. With any luck, her old car wouldn't break down on the return trip and they'd be home within a few days.

She'd have to call Tom and see if she still had a job. Once home she planned to look into community college courses in business. She liked working in an office. If she could find the time, she'd like to learn more.

Gently folding her business suit, she brushed her fingers over the soft material. It would be perfect for interviews, once she had some skills. Every time she wore it, she'd remember Mitch and their whirlwind trip to Los Angeles.

Would Mitch give her a reference?

"What are you doing?"

Mitch stood in the doorway holding a Stetson in one hand. His jeans were dusty, his boots muddy. Ginny could smell horses and cattle from where she stood. And her heart flipped over.

"Packing. Helen is back."

"I saw her before I went out to check on the bore that's giving us trouble. She said you had come to the office, but she hadn't needed help." He looked at the opened suitcase. "Leaving?"

"I thought it best. You don't need me anymore now that Helen's here. I'll take Joey in to Dallas tomorrow for the follow-up visit to the surgeon, then head for home."

He stared at her for a long moment. Ginny wanted to fidget under his gaze, but held onto her composure. Unable to meet his eyes, however, she resumed folding and packing.

"Don't go." Mitch said in such a low voice she thought she had imagined it.

"What?" She looked up. He was studying the carpet.

"Don't go. Stay here. We'll find something for you to do."

She hadn't imagined it. "Like what? I'm no cowboy. And we both know I was a makeshift secretary. I'd need more training if I wanted to do that full-time. You don't need more than Helen here. Each office has a full staff, there'd be nothing for me to do."

"We'll find something."

"I can't stay. We've imposed enough." And she didn't want to feel like a charity case. She hoped she'd pulled her weight at the office. But there was nothing left for her to do.

"You haven't imposed. Joey likes it here. Emaline likes having him around. He's almost old enough to have a pony."

"Which I can't afford." Why was he making it so hard?

"But I can," Mitch said.

She shook her head at his stubbornness and arrogance. Just because he could, didn't make it right for her to accept. "We are already in your debt for the operation."

"You helped me out when I needed it. Consider us even."

Ginny did not consider them even, but she wasn't going to argue with him. Once home, she'd figure out how much she could pay each week and send the money.

"You didn't get to go to college. Stay and take some classes. See if you still want to be an architect. Joey can start school in Tumbleweed in the fall. Emaline and Rosita could watch him afternoons."

"Mitch, I can't stay. I don't have a job, no income. My savings won't last for long and I can't let you foot the bill for my schooling." Joey's operation was one thing, she'd do anything for her son, even swallow her pride. But Mitch was talking something totally different now.

"You could stay and go to college if you married me."

CHAPTER NINE

Now she knew she was hallucinating. She stared at him, hope blossoming. *Marriage? To Mitch?*

She cleared her throat. "Marriage?"

He meet her eyes and nodded. "Marry me and stay here in Tumbleweed. Joey loves the ranch. You like it here, you said so."

A thousand questions flooded Ginny's mind. But the happiness that exploded drove every one away. Mitch wanted her to stay—enough to marry her!

She held his gaze as she walked toward him. "Are you sure?" Once, long ago, she'd thought a man would want to marry her, instead, he'd vanished from her life completely. Now she was grateful. The love she felt for Mitch was far stronger than any she'd imagined for Joey's father. But marriage—it had been the last thing she'd expected.

He reached for her when she came near, pulling her into his embrace.

"I'm dusty and sweaty from riding," he said, looking down into her eyes.

"I don't mind a bit," she said, reaching up to kiss him.

Would she always be breathless around him, always become instantly inflamed by his kisses? She hoped so.

Winding her arms around his neck, she kissed him, pouring as much of her love into the embrace as she could. She loved him and he loved her. They were going to spend their lives together!

Wait until she told Joey. And Emaline. And Maggie.

''I love you, Mitch,'' she whispered against his mouth.

He pulled back a bit. ''Then it's settled. We'll get married and you'll stay here. Let me take a quick shower and then we'll tell the others,'' he said, brushing his thumb across Ginny's damp lips. ''Joey will be delighted, I suspect.''

Ginny smiled, her arms still looped around his neck. He was hers! She could touch him whenever she wanted. See him whenever she wanted. She wished she could run up to the rooftop and shout the news to the world! Take an ad out in every daily paper in the country, plaster billboards with the news.

''I'm sure he'll be thrilled. But he'll pester you to death now to let him be a cowboy,'' she said, pleased he included Joey in the arrangement.

She had to imagine the pain that flickered in his eyes. This was a joyful occasion.

He nodded, gently pulling her arms down. ''I'll meet you for lunch and we'll tell Emaline and Joey together.''

Ginny watched him walk down the hall to his own room, wishing she dare follow him. She'd love to be there when he came out of the shower. Talk while he dressed. Their lovemaking in Los Angeles had been wonderful, how much more would it be now that they were planning to share the rest of their lives together?

She turned back to her bed and quickly unpacked.

The next move would be to Mitch's room and she wouldn't need the suitcase for that.

Of course, there were her things in Florida. Maybe he'd like to take their honeymoon there and pack up her apartment. It didn't sound that romantic, but it would be practical.

She brushed her hair, her thoughts spinning. How soon could they marry? Would he stay at the ranch more, or move them to his penthouse in Dallas? Staring at the bright color in her face she just grinned, letting the delight blossom in her heart. *Mitch loved her.*

Or did he?

She paused, brush suspended midair, suddenly realizing he had never said the words.

But surely a man didn't ask a woman to marry him if he didn't love her. Guys weren't as mushy as women, hadn't she always heard that? Of course he loved her.

She stared at herself in the mirror, doubts crowded in. He had to love her. She loved him so much she couldn't stand it if he didn't love her back. But he hadn't said the words. And she had—loud and clear.

Was he shy. She almost laughed, except fear gripped her. She couldn't picture Mitch shy about anything. So why hadn't he said the word back?

Because he didn't love her. He was still in love with his first wife. Ginny was just—what? A convenience? Or was he offering her a place to live for some other reason?

Mitch made the announcement as soon as they were seated, with Rosita present. Ginny hadn't had a chance to talk to him and couldn't now with everyone bubbling over with the news. But later, she'd corner him later and get some answers. In the meantime, she put on a happy face and tried not to let the doubts and fears gain dominance.

"Oh, my dear," Emaline rose instantly and came to give Ginny a hug. "I'm so delighted." She moved to kiss her nephew and then Joey.

"Are you my daddy now?" Joey asked.

"I'll be your stepfather," Mitch replied.

"And we get to live here forever and ever?" Joey persisted.

"Yes, forever and ever."

"Can I have a pony?"

Ginny laughed. "I knew it. We'll wait to discuss that later." Something else to talk over when they were alone.

"I wish you much happiness, Señor, Señorita," Rosita said, her face wreathed in smiles.

"My goodness, after lunch, Ginny, you and Rosita and I will have to get together to begin wedding plans," Emaline said when she resumed her seat. "A garden wedding do you think? Or since you'll probably become a member of our church would you rather have it there? Oh dear, you didn't want to have it in Florida, did you?"

"We'll probably have a judge marry us," Mitch said, reaching for the plate of biscuits.

Three pairs of eyes swung to him in dismay.

He looked up. "No?"

"It's Ginny's wedding, I think she should decide," Emaline said primly.

"It's my wedding, too," Mitch said.

"I know, dear, but a second for you. This is her first."

"And only one, I hope," she murmured, struck by the questions that wouldn't leave. Why had he asked her? It was likely Mitch didn't want to do anything to remind him of his first wedding. Had it been a garden wedding? Or a formal affair held in the church? He never spoke about Marlisse and rarely about Daisy. For a moment the sunshine seemed dimmer. They needed to discuss this in private and soon.

"We'll decide what we want and then make plans," Ginny said. "He just asked me, there are a thousand things to decide. Let us get used to the idea first."

"Very well, but it's already June, and a summer wedding is so lovely," Emaline said.

"Can I have a dog?" Joey asked, bored with the discussion about weddings.

"We'll see," Mitch said.

"Yea!"

Mitch raised an eyebrow and looked at Ginny. She shrugged.

"It's almost a sure thing if I say I'll see," she explained.

As soon as lunch was finished, Mitch rose and excused himself with having to go to the office. He brushed a kiss on Ginny's cheek. "I need to talk to you," she said.

"We can talk after dinner, just the two of us."

"Sounds good," she said, her heart rate increased with his casual kiss. Just as if they were already old, married folks. She was the luckiest woman on the face of the earth! For a few hours she kept that thought in the forefront, refusing to dwell on the doubts.

After dinner, Ginny supervised Joey's bath, careful not to let his head get wet, nor let him move suddenly which could cause a problem with the healing eye. Once he was in bed, they talked for a while about the changes in their lives. He didn't mind leaving the ocean if he could have a dog and a pony and one day go on roundups.

Ginny was delighted her son took to the changes, but wondered how strong the bond with Mitch would become. Would he have time for Joey? Or constantly be drawn to working long hours as he had in the weeks they'd lived at the ranch?

Once Joey was settled for the night, Ginny went to find Mitch. Time to talk. She wandered down to the study. Emaline had already returned to her cottage for the evening. Rosita was in her room, so it would be just the two of them, with no chance of interruption. Ginny's heart sped up in anticipation of what the two of them might find to do that went beyond discussion.

She paused in the doorway, studying the man she loved. His shoulders were broad, strong enough to support the weight of the world, she thought whimsically. His dark hair beckoned. She wanted to run her fingers through it, claiming him as hers.

He was studying a photograph. Curious, Ginny entered the room and crossed to the desk.

He looked up, his face shuttered.

"Hi," she said softly, her eyes on the picture. It was of a young girl. "Is that Daisy?"

He nodded and held the photo out for her inspection. She had been a darling child, bright and laughing in the pose. Ginny felt a clutch of sadness at the thought of this happy life being cut so short. She handed it back.

"She was beautiful," she said softly. "Do you have other pictures?"

He nodded, slipping the photograph into the top drawer of the desk.

"Ask Emaline. She kept them all. She can show you the whole clan. I'm sure she plans to invite them all to the wedding."

Ginny sat gingerly on the edge of the desk. "If you want to just stand up in front of a judge, that would work for me." She had given up dreams of a white dress and formal church wedding after Joey's father had vanished. The wedding wasn't what was important to her, the marriage was.

Mitch held out his hand, and Ginny took it. He drew her over to him and settled her in his lap, resting his head on the softness of her hair. He meant to go through with the wedding. Bleakly he gazed off into space, holding one woman, thinking of another wedding. Of the parties, the excitement, the surety they both had of love everlasting.

Ginny deserved the same excitement, the same happiness. She didn't know many people in Texas. It wouldn't be the same. But he wanted her to be happy. To have memories she could cherish in the years to come.

"What do you think of a garden wedding," he asked. "Emaline will invite a few thousand guests

and we could have an old-fashioned Texas-style barbecue for a reception.''

''A few thousand? You're joking, right?'' The uncertainty in Ginny's voice touched him. And once
again affirmed he had made the right decision.

''You know Emaline, she never met anyone who
wasn't an instant friend. But I do suspect thousands
is a bit of an exaggeration. Maybe only several hundred. Once you get all the cousins and family, the
entire town, and my business associates, it'll be a
crowd. You'll have friends you want to invite.''

''Not many, and I doubt they'll be able to come to
Texas anyway,'' she said slowly.

''Hey, for your wedding, we'll send them airline
tickets.''

She shook her head. ''Too expensive.''

Mitch wanted to tell her she never need worry
about money again. After years of fending off relatives and acquaintances interested in that money,
Ginny was a refreshing change. Was that the reason
he wanted to shower her with anything she desired?

Or was it to make up for the lack in him? She
wanted hearts and flowers and love everlasting, and
he had only a home to offer and the ability to provide
for her son. He hoped it would be enough. In the
meantime, he'd get Helen to find out more about
Ginny's closest friends and make the arrangements—
once they decided on a wedding date.

''How soon would you like to get married?'' he
asked.

''Tomorrow,'' she replied promptly. ''If you're
sure.''

''Why wouldn't I be?'' he asked.

"I don't know." She was afraid to ask if he loved her. What if he didn't? She wasn't sure she could face that.

"Why do you want to marry me, Mitch?" she asked softly.

"Why do people normally marry—to spend time together, to share their lives."

"I love you, but you've never said that back to me. You don't say it at Emaline either."

"I care for my aunt."

"And me?"

"And you."

"Love?"

"Let's not get into some philosophical discussion about love and other emotions," he said. "We'll be married, I will be pledging my life to yours. You'll have stability, a home, and a place Joey can grow up. I'll do my best by both of you."

Ginny felt a clutch in her heart. He was offering her more than she ever expected—was it enough? Did he love her and just not want to say the words? Or had he closed himself off so much that the offer of a home was all he had to give?

What should she do? Could she take him on those terms?

"Emaline is right, we want to do this properly. We'll invite the town, friends, family and have the wedding in the garden. I'll get some of the men to expand the grassy area. If we get sod, we can have it ready by the time our wedding date rolls around. How about August first?"

"If you're sure," she said, nestled against his chest. Maybe men just weren't as vocal about their feelings. He hadn't had to ask her. Things could turn out for the best.

And she wanted it so much, how could it be wrong?

"A pretty wedding dress for you, and new clothes for Joey. Not a suit, but western attire, what do you think?"

"He'll love it. Especially if you suggest it."

She rubbed her fingertips across his biceps. She hadn't forgotten one moment of their time in Los Angeles. Soon they'd have all their nights together. This was the right step. He wouldn't have asked if he didn't want her.

"And I suggest you get a beautiful dress, white if you like," he said.

"With a four-year-old boy?"

"Off white, then, but feminine and especially made for you."

"We'll see."

"Good, that means yes."

Ginny tipped back her head to look at him. She moved her hand to his cheek, pressing gently. He leaned forward and kissed her. How long before he would take her upstairs to his bed? She wanted something tangible to quell all the doubts that still lingered.

The next morning Ginny, Emaline and Rosita gathered in the kitchen early. Ginny and Emaline were taking Joey in for a follow-up visit to the surgeon at ten. The women were planning on which shops to visit and what to look for now that the date and type of wedding had been decided.

As they drove into Dallas, Ginny wished Mitch had

come with them. Not that she needed him, but wished he could have shared the moment the surgeon unwrapped Joey's eye and both eyes stared at her normally.

There was still therapy to do, corrective lenses to wear until the eyes grew used to tracking together, but Joey was amenable to it all. His good mood lasted throughout the afternoon when Emaline directed them to shop after shop, to a caterer and to two florists, looking for the perfect items for the wedding.

Ginny wanted to check out some of the stores in Tumbleweed before making her final decisions, but she enjoyed the glamor of the clothes, the tastes of the proposed tidbits from the caterer. The main barbecue would be handled by the ranch hands, Emaline said.

Joey fell asleep on the ride back to the ranch.

Ginny was almost as tired when they arrived home. She didn't know how Emaline managed, the woman was decades older, but she seemed as energetic and raring to go as ever. Wistfully she wished she could sleep as Joey had. But there wouldn't be time before dinner for a nap.

At the evening meal, Mitch suggested they go into Tumbleweed in the morning.

"Don't you have work to do?" Ginny asked.

"I want us to choose rings."

"Splendid! I wondered when you'd get around to that, nephew. Seems to me you had the ring in hand when you proposed to Marlisse," Emaline said.

"I wasn't as uncertain of Marlisse's answer as I was of Ginny's," Mitch said easily. "We'll look at the jewelers in town. If you don't see something you like we can go into Dallas.''

''I'm sure they'll have just the right ring in Tumbleweed.'' Ginny was thrilled he wanted to buy an engagement ring. He did care, just didn't say the words. It wasn't that long until the wedding. A plain gold band would have suited her. To have an engagement ring to show the world had to mean something.

''We'll have lunch in town.''

''To celebrate. Actually, maybe you two should plan a dinner in Dallas. I'm sure the restaurants there are much better than the ones we have in Tumbleweed,'' Emaline said. ''I could watch Joey for you. We could have a nice sleep over at my cottage, would you like that, Joey?''

The little boy nodded agreeably.

''We could rent a movie and watch it with popcorn and then he could sleep in Grandpa Eli's feather bed. That's a treat I remember from my girlhood.''

Ginny smiled as Joey asked questions about the feather bed. His eyes grew bigger as Emaline told about plucking goose down from geese that grandpa Eli had raised and stuffing them in the ticking. She went on to tell about the time the ticking split and feathers went everywhere.

Ginny looked to Mitch to share her delight, only to find he seemed miles away, totally unaware of Emaline's story.

When he saw her gaze, he looked away.

''So shall I plan on Joey for tomorrow night?'' Emaline asked, at the end of her story.

''Another time we'll take you up on it, but tomorrow, lunch will have to suffice,'' Mitch said, rising. He left the table, his plate still half full.

After Joey had been put to bed, and Emaline returned home, Ginny went downstairs to the study. Mitch retired there every evening after dinner. Would he continue to do so once they were married or would the two of them share quiet evenings together?

"Am I interrupting?" she asked from the doorway.

"Not at all. Come in." Mitch pressed a few buttons on his computer keyboard and shut down the program. "I was just checking my e-mail. Which I can as easily do in the morning. Tell me more about what the doctor said about Joey's prognosis."

Ginny wished he'd hold out his hand and draw her into his lap again, but he merely leaned back in his chair and waited.

She sat on one of the other chairs near the desk and told him about her day, then asked about his. For a while the conversation flowed.

When it wound down, Ginny hesitated to ask any of the myriad of questions she had. There was so much about Mitch she wanted to know—everything in fact. Of course she had the rest of her life to find the answers, but she was impatient, wanting to know it all right now!

She rested her head on the back of the chair, content that she had been able to talk with him so easily. Maybe the other questions would just come up naturally.

"Tired?" Mitch asked.

"I am a little," she admitted. "Emaline has lots more energy than I have. I think we visited half the stores in Dallas, and she would have covered the other half if we had had time.''

Mitch rose and crossed over to her, planting his hands on either arm of her chair. ''Come to bed with me,'' he said.

Ginny gazed up into his dark eyes, seeing desire blatantly displayed.

''I'd love to,'' she said simply.

When Ginny awoke the next morning, Mitch had already left. Drowsily, she reached for his pillow, drinking in his scent, holding it against her, the cotton pillowcase cool against her bare skin. She smiled dreamily. It was nothing like the hot body that had kept her warm all night long.

After they had made love, they had talked, discussing mundane things like enrolling Joey in kindergarten and who would take him to the bus stop out on the highway each morning. Or if she wanted to redecorate some or all of the house, which Ginny had never even considered.

Now that morning arrived, she remembered they were going to Tumbleweed to get a ring. She felt she glowed with happiness. What kind of ring would Mitch want her to have? She liked simple settings. None of his tastes were ostentatious, so they'd probably easily agree on the ring.

Would he wear a wedding ring as well? She'd like that. Feeling possessive, she wanted the entire world to know he was hers!

She could spend the entire morning in bed dreaming about Mitch and their lives together, but she had to get up. Joey would awaken soon and wonder where she was if she wasn't in her room.

Time enough for him to get used to her sleeping with Mitch once they were married.

As she rose and dressed in yesterday's clothing she wondered when *she* would get used to sleeping in his bed.

After a quick shower and change of clothes, Ginny went to see to Joey. She wished she had something else to wear, but jeans would have to do. The suit from her Los Angeles trip was just too dressy for casual Tumbleweed, and she hadn't brought anything else from Florida.

As ten o'clock approached, Ginny grew nervous. This would be the first time anyone outside the immediate family knew of Mitch's coming marriage. How would his neighbors and friends take it? They had all known his first wife and daughter. Would they draw comparisons?

Ginny wished she knew more about Marlisse and the circumstance of Mitch's marriage.

"Don't be silly," she told herself as she walked out into the sunshine. "He asked me to marry him, not the other way around."

Entering the office, Ginny smiled at Helen. She noticed Mitch's office door was closed. "Is Mitch ready?"

"I believe so. He told me he'd be gone most of the day. I didn't have a chance to offer my best wishes yesterday. I hope you both will be happy." She rang the intercom and told Mitch that Ginny was waiting to see him.

"We're buying rings," Ginny said, trying for a friendly note.

Helen looked up and nodded. "So he said. Get a big one, he's good for it."

Ginny wandered to the door, waiting. She had called Maggie first thing yesterday to share her news. Then called Tom to tell him she wouldn't be returning to Florida to live and formally giving notice to quit. What else did she need to deal with before the date?

"Ready?" Mitch came from his office. Ginny smiled, feeling that thrill she did every time she saw him. Today it felt even stronger knowing one day they would be married and starting life together.

"We get back late this afternoon," he told Helen.

Ginny noticed he wore jeans as well. Had he done so deliberately to put her at ease? Mitch could be dictatorial sometimes, but he also could be surprisingly thoughtful. A complex man she was marrying.

Just before they reached town, Ginny asked if he would wear a wedding ring.

"If you want me to," he replied.

She wanted to ask if he had with Marlisse, but couldn't, make herself say the words. It really didn't matter. This was their marriage, not his first one. Whether they did things the same or differently, it only mattered that they did what they wanted.

The jeweler looked surprised when Mitch told him what he wanted. The glance at Ginny had her once again feeling inadequate and lacking. But she forgot it all when the man spread out a rainbow of rings on the black velvet drop cloth. The diamonds sparkled in the light. The few other precious stones contrasted sharply with the shimmering brilliance of the diamonds.

Mitch picked one and held it for Ginny's inspection. "Do you like this one?"

"It's nice."

"Lacks a ringing endorsement," he said, placing it back on the velvet. "Which do you prefer?"

She studied the display, reaching out for the simple solitary diamond in a plain gold setting. "This one." Despite Helen's words, Ginny wanted a ring she loved, not one to show off. She'd be wearing it all her life.

He nodded to the jeweler. "We'd like to see matching wedding rings, as well."

They looked at the rings, discussing what they liked and didn't like, finally choosing matching bands with a braided motif. Somehow the morning fell flat.

Ginny didn't know why, she should be thrilled to be choosing rings for a lifetime. Maybe it was the jeweler's supercilious attitude, or Mitch's lack of emotion. Somehow there was no spark, no excitement.

And she couldn't even have her engagement ring today, it had to be sized to fit her smaller finger.

Still, she reminded herself as they left the shop, it was the marriage that counted, not the trappings.

Mitch took her to the Cattlemen's Club, one of the nicest restaurants in Tumbleweed. It was crowded with ranchers and local businessmen, but the hostess found a quiet table for them. As they wound through the main dining room, several people called greetings to Mitch. He returned them all, not stopping to introduce Ginny.

After they were seated, he looked at her. "Time enough to get to know everyone without have to explain to everyone we meet today," he said. Glancing around the room, he continued, "Most of them will be at the wedding."

"It'll probably take me months to get everyone straight."

A familiar person approached. Ginny had no trouble getting Gloria straight. She braced herself, but the woman virtually ignored her.

"Mitch, darling. I didn't know you were coming in to town today." With a dismissing glance at Ginny, she smiled warmly at him. "Taking your little secretary out to lunch? How nice."

Mitch had risen when she reached the table, now he smiled, but Ginny noticed there was no warmth in his gaze.

"Helen has returned, Ginny is no longer working as my secretary."

"Oh?" Gloria looked surprised, but it was nothing to her expression when he added, "Ginny and I are celebrating our engagement. We're to be married in August. You and your family will receive an invitation, of course."

"I didn't even know you were dating again," Gloria blurted. Recovering quickly, she forced a smile on her face and offered congratulations. Once she resumed her seat several tables away, Mitch sat down.

Technically, Ginny thought as she perused the menu, this was probably their first date. Unless she counted the dinner and dancing at the business meal in Los Angeles. No wonder Gloria hadn't heard he was dating.

From the way people began to look their way, Ginny knew Gloria was already spreading the news. But Mitch seemed totally oblivious. Taking her cue from him, she ignored the other diners and concentrated on Mitch.

As he had said, this was to celebrate their engagement, putting on a bright smile, she set out to celebrate.

They returned home in the late afternoon and Mitch headed for the office.

"I have time to go over a few things with Helen," he said, glancing at his watch. "I'll see you at dinner."

Ginny looked for Joey, but when she didn't find him in his room, she went to check with Rosita.

"He's over at the cottage with Señorita Emaline. She was going to let him take a nap in that feather bed she has. I guess her stories last night made him want to sleep in it and she dotes on him. He's a lucky boy."

"We both are," Ginny said. Joey would have an extended family now, with Emaline, and the rest of Mitch's family. Aunts, uncles, cousins. Grandparents. How would his family feel about this marriage? She hadn't even met his parents. It was a lot to think about.

Ginny walked the short distance to Emaline's cottage. She had never been inside and was enchanted when invited in. It looked like a doll's house, with feminine Queen Anne furniture, lacy curtains and colorful pillows everywhere. It suited Emaline to a T.

Pictures crowded the living room walls, some of Mitch, other of family members she didn't as yet know. Knickknacks cluttered the tabletops and shelves, from delicate crystals, to fine bone china, to sturdier snuffboxes and carved wooden figures.

Emaline was delighted to see Ginny, and wanted to hear all about the rings they'd chosen. She was disappointed Ginny wasn't wearing the engagement ring yet.

Since Joey was still napping, she fixed them both lemonade and brought cookies into the front room, as she called it.

Ginny crossed the room to help with the tray. She had been looking at the photographs.

''These are wonderful, all relatives? Some of the pictures look a hundred years old.''

''They are. My great-great-grandparents are in that stilted one there,'' Emaline said, pointing to one with two unsmiling individuals dress in somber black.

''I have albums full of old pictures. I'm the only one in the family who wants them all. When everyone gets together, we spend hours going over the old albums and talking about our ancestors. But then they leave them with me. I have sorted most of them and put them in albums.''

''You have pictures of Daisy, Mitch said. Could I see?''

''Oh, yes. She was such a darling child. I don't guess any of us will ever entirely get over her untimely death.''

Ginny took a sip of her lemonade while Emaline pulled a thick album from the lower shelf. She flipped it toward the end, and pointed at the sweet little girl who smiled so sunnily into the camera.

Mitch's daughter. Ginny felt a pang of sadness at

the loss. How did he bear it? She didn't think she could ever endure Joey's death.

Idly flipping through the photos, she came across one with Mitch and a tall brunette, both smiling. She paused, he looked younger, different—so happy. That must be Marlisse. Ginny studied the photo. She and Marlisse were nothing alike. At least he wasn't marrying her because she resembled his first wife. Marlisse had been closer to Mitch in age. Her healthy outdoor glow attested to her love of ranch work. Hadn't he known her all his life?

"I believe I hear Joey, I'll go check," Emaline said. She hurried down the hall. Ginny turned the pages again, not wanting to dwell on a woman long gone. Not wanting to think about comparing herself with Mitch's first love.

Mitch's only love? The insidious thought wouldn't be squelched.

She turned the page when she heard Emaline returning, her eyes instantly focused on the familiar face. Her heart almost stopped.

"It's Joey's father!" she said in stunned amazement.

CHAPTER TEN

"OH NO, dear, that can't be," Emaline said, looking over Ginny's shoulder at the eight by ten wedding photograph filling the page.

"That's Mitch's cousin Sam. Samuel Houston Holden. He just got married a year or so ago to the sweetest girl, Sara Anne Pembroke. They live in Austin. They haven't even started a family yet. And his hair is brown, not blond. Didn't you say Joey's father was blond?"

"His hair is darker, and he has a mustache now, but it's him. He told me he was John Mitchell Holden." Ginny was sure of it. The same sexy arrogance shone in the picture. The way he held his head, the eyes that were exactly like Joey's. It was the man she'd known as John Mitchell Holden five years ago on the beach at Fort Lauderdale.

A cousin of Mitch's. Of course, who better to know about John Mitchell Holden and the ranch than a family member who had known him all his life? But why had he used Mitch's name instead of his own?

"Oh dear. I don't know what Mitch'll say," Emaline said.

Ginny studied the picture, expecting to feel something. But there was nothing. No hurt, no pain, no regrets. Any feelings she had once held for this man had faded over the years. She loved Mitch totally and completely. Staring at this face, she felt as if she only knew him slightly, from another world. He had no place in her life, in Joey's life. She was free of any spell he'd once held.

She looked up at Emaline. "Don't tell him anything. He doesn't need to know."

"Oh, but he does, dear. Otherwise we'd invite Sam to the wedding and think how awkward that would be," Emaline said definitely worried.

Grimly, Ginny nodded. Awkward didn't begin to describe it. How could she marry into the family unless Mitch knew the truth. Would it wreck his relationship with his cousin? What of their own relationship? How would he feel knowing she'd once loved his cousin?

Ginny knew Emaline had already told Mitch by the way he stared at Joey during dinner—and by the curt responses to any overtures on her part. Even Emaline seemed subdued. Rosita eyed them curiously as she served the meal. But nothing was said in front of Joey.

Ginny felt as if they had already set a pattern for evenings. She'd put Joey to bed, then wander down to Mitch's study where they'd spend time together. Emaline usually left right before Joey went to bed, so the remainder of the evening belonged to her and Mitch. They could discuss the latest turn, decide what they would do. Her heart beating fast, she headed for the study.

Tonight she heard him talking as she approached the door. It was almost closed, but hadn't caught. Did he have a visitor?

"…then let me hypothesize. You died your hair

blond, took off for Florida on spring break when your mother and I thought you were studying to complete your course work with a passing grade. You used *my name* so no one would find out. What did you do, hock something to come up with the money?''

There was a silence. Ginny could almost feel the waves of frustration and anger. She pressed closer, knowing she shouldn't be eavesdropping, but unable to resist. Mitch was talking to his cousin.

''Water under the bridge, huh. Did you never think there would be consequences to your actions?''

Another moment of silence. She wished she could hear the other person. Did he have regrets? Had it only been a careless fling for him? Would he want to know his son?

''Dammit Sammy, I've bailed you out of trouble a dozen times since your father died. You drove your mother to distraction with your antics, always expecting someone else to pull your chestnuts from the fire. I thought you'd turned around that last time. What of the promises you made to her? To me?''

Another silence. Ginny's heart pounded. She closed her eyes, wishing with all her heart that she had never seen the picture, that she had never said the fateful words aloud, or that Emaline had not returned at that very moment.

''Yeah, well old son, one of those wild oats is in my house right now. Along with his mother. Remember her? Ginny Morgan? Pretty blond with a figure that makes a man drool?''

Ginny hardly heard the compliment. Why had Mitch called his cousin? Shouldn't he have discussed things with her first? They could have decided together how to handle the situation. Decided whether to invite Sam to the wedding or not. Though she supposed that was a temporary measure. There were years of family events ahead of them. They needed to decide how to handle them all.

"While you were graduating from the university through the strings your mother and I pulled, Ginny was giving up hope of college and scrambling around to take care of your son…. That counts for nothing. Her aunt died. So it was just Ginny and Joey—and all the problems of being a single parent with no education to speak of…."

"I don't know what I want you to do, but I'm so mad I could spit. When are you going to take responsibility for your life, for your choices and for your mistakes? I'm tired of bailing you out of scrapes." Mitch hard voice sent shivers up Ginny's back. She hoped he never got that angry with her.

She caught her breath as the pain hit her. Was that what he was doing? Bailing her out? Providing a place for her because…because why? For Joey? In memory of Daisy? Not because he loved her. He hadn't once told her so. And now, he had yet to mention to his cousin their upcoming wedding. Instead he was demanding his cousin take responsibility—to relieve him of the need?

Was she living a lie?

No wonder she couldn't believe Mitch loved her. He didn't, and she'd known it deep inside.

Ginny turned and almost stumbled. She froze afraid Mitch had heard her. He mustn't know she overheard his conversation. He must never suspect.

Quietly she made her way back upstairs, to her

room. Closing the door softly behind her, she leaned against it, feeling old and tired and so dispirited she couldn't even begin to imagine her future.

Maybe there'd been a reason the ring hadn't been ready today—it was never to be hers.

Maybe there'd been a reason Mitch hadn't told anyone, he had hoped something would turn up so his impetuous proposal would become moot.

Did he expect Sam to sweep in and take her and Joey off with him? She was sure his wife would have something to say to that.

Everything was a mess. Slowly she crossed the room and eased down on the bed, too distraught for tears, she gazed dried-eyed off into the darkness, wondering what was the best thing to do.

She and Joey couldn't stay, not now—knowing Mitch didn't really love her, didn't really want to marry her. They'd have to return to Florida. The sooner the better. Before any further plans were made, or any further action taken for a wedding that would never take place.

In the morning. They'd leave in the morning.

Sometime later Mitch knocked softly on her door. Ginny didn't move. Even if he opened the door, he'd see the room was dark and assume she was asleep. After a moment, she heard him move away.

Goodbye, she silently called after him. *Goodbye, my love.*

Ginny slept fitfully during the night. When dawn lightened the sky, she rose, and went to shower and change. Sleeping in her clothes had been uncomfortable, but she'd hardly noticed.

Once dressed, she quietly set about packing. She'd done this before, only this time there'd be no man standing in the doorway asking her to stay.

She almost cringed remembering how happy she'd been when he'd asked her to marry him.

Why hadn't she realized at the time it was third choice? He'd first offered her a job, then a chance at schooling. She still didn't understand why he felt he had to marry her, but she wished she'd gone with her instincts at the time that as a proposal, it had fallen a little short of perfection.

She had noticed when buying the rings. But she had wanted it too much to pay attention to obvious signs. Just as she had five years ago when Aunt Edith warned her to be careful. She was too trusting and too impetuous. Maybe this time she'd learn that lesson.

Her car was parked in back. When she heard Joey moving around, she went to get him dressed and then sent him down to see about breakfast. Rosita loved pampering him. Let him have one last meal before they departed. Once he scampered down the stairs, she quickly packed his things.

She wrote a short note and left it in the study where Mitch would see it. She assured him she would repay the cost of the surgery, and thanked him for all he'd done for them both. Taking both suitcases to the car, she put them in the trunk, fairly certain no one had seen her.

She joined Joey for breakfast, complimenting Rosita on her cooking, and thanking her for all she'd done for them.

"My pleasure. If things don't go the way you want,

you must tell me. A woman takes more interest in how her own house is run than a man, I think. You'll be in charge. I do hope you will keep me on.''

Ginny nodded, knowing there would never be a change. Even if Rosita didn't run things perfectly, Ginny wouldn't be here to notice. ''You run this home, Rosita, nothing will ever change that,'' Ginny said, knowing how true it was.

After breakfast, Ginny took Joey outside. ''We need to have a talk, Joey. And we need to drive in our car,'' she said.

''Okay.''

Ginny had to get his car seat from Mitch's sedan, and she almost held her breath lest someone see her and ask what she was doing, but the ranch was quiet. The cowboys were out on the range, and Mitch and Helen were in the office on the other side of the house. Emaline didn't usually come over to the big house until closer to lunchtime.

Ginny would miss her. She regretted not being able to tell her goodbye. But she dare not risk it. She'd write and make sure Joey sent a picture or something.

As they drove down the driveway, Ginny did all she could to keep her feelings numb. Turning her back on the man she loved was the hardest thing she had ever done. But she couldn't live where love didn't bloom.

By the time they stopped for the night, Ginny's stoicism had broken. Once a cranky, confused and unhappy Joey was asleep, she took a shower and cried until the water ran cold. Slipping into her nightshirt, she climbed into bed, falling asleep almost as soon as her head hit the pillow. She hated leaving, but hated the thought of living with Mitch when he didn't love her even more. Had he been bailing her out as he obviously was used to doing with his cousin? She refused to be a burden.

The next morning she felt groggy and cranky herself. Her eyes were swollen from her crying and her energy level flagging. But her determination never wavered.

She pushed on eastward, despite Joey's demands to return to the ranch. She tried over and over to explain to him they had to return home, but he was inconsolable. He wanted to see Mitch, to see Emaline, to play with the dogs and pet the horses. To learn to ride and get his own pony. And learn to become a cowboy.

Through Louisiana, Mississippi and Alabama she drove, trying to ignore her son's tearful pleas, and the demands of her own heart. Maybe she should have stayed. Even half a loaf was better than nothing, wasn't it? Even if Mitch didn't love her, she loved him, wouldn't that have been enough?

Another night of tears and Ginny was ready to do anything to get Joey to stop urging her to do what she wanted to do more than anything. Finally she bribed him. If he'd stop talking about the ranch and the people who lived there and stopped pressuring her to return, she'd get him a puppy when they reached home.

It worked like a charm. Too bad she couldn't find the same solace in the thought of a new family member.

Then, as if programmed to add to her frustration

and unhappiness, the car broke down just after reaching the Florida state lines. Another day waiting for a part, and Ginny was ready to tear her hair. All she wanted was the sanctuary of her home

On the sixth day they reached Fort Lauderdale. Ginny was exhausted. An afternoon thundershower forced them to close the windows. Since the car didn't have working air-conditioning, she was growing hotter and damp with perspiration and humidity. The drive had been a strain. She wanted a shower, and a quick dinner, then bed. Tomorrow was soon enough to sort through things and make plans.

Tears threatened again when she thought of plans she'd made with Mitch. But she resolutely put that behind her.

She'd call Maggie first thing. Her friend would help. And once she was back at work, engulfed in normal routine things, she'd quickly forget about Mitch Holden and the promise he'd once held.

She pulled into her designated parking place and stopped. Once again they'd have to get out in the rain. She still didn't have an umbrella. No matter. This time they could change once they got inside.

She'd get the bags later. Right now she just wanted the sanctuary of their apartment.

When she and Joey quickly rounded the side of the building to reach the front door without becoming totally soaked, he suddenly pulled away, running ahead of her, splashing through puddles, yelling.

"It's Mitch. He's come to get us!"

Ginny stopped, staring. The rain poured down, wetting her shirt, her hair, her bare legs beneath her shorts. But she couldn't move. It was Mitch.

He rose from the top step and reached down to swing Joey up and hug him. "Howdy, partner. You doing okay?" he asked, his eyes immediately moving to find Ginny.

She slowly walked forward. What in the world was he doing here? Her heart pounded. She felt light-headed. Mitch, here. She wanted to run into his arms and have him hold her forever. But caution prevailed. She'd made her decision, nothing had changed.

"We missed you, Mitch. But Mommy is getting me a puppy, one that can come in the house. Can he come in your house? I want him to sleep on my bed with me, but she said no, he had to stary on the floor. But he can come inside, can't he?" Joey was talking almost as much as Emaline did.

Mitch said, "We'll see." He leaned over to put Joey down, his eyes capturing Ginny's as he walked toward her.

"What are you doing here?" she asked afraid to believe her eyes.

"First things first," he said, pulling her into his arms and kissing her hard.

She didn't know whether to feel chastised or cherished when he ended the kiss. She knew she felt totally bemused with the rain pouring down, the thunder rumbling in the distance and her heart racing.

"Did you have car trouble?" he asked.

"Of course," she said with a sigh.

"I've been here two days. I thought I gave you enough time to get home if you didn't have car trouble, but I thought you had to have been held up by something. I worry about you in that car."

"We're fine. Why are you here?"

"Why wouldn't I be, you're here."

"I left you a note."

"Don't you think I deserve more than a short note? We're getting married, Ginny. Surely you can do better than that."

The rain bounced off the pavement, the scent of wet asphalt filled her senses.

"We're getting wet," she said, wishing he was right—that they were still getting married. She watched him warily.

"So invite me inside."

It was the least she could do. Hadn't he taken her in when she knocked on his door in the rain? It wasn't quite déjà vu, he wasn't sick. She couldn't have stood it if he stayed beyond the length of time it would take her to explain. She just hoped she could do so without making a total idiot of herself blubbering about love and devotion and obligations and all.

As soon as they entered her apartment, she knew it had been a mistake. Mitch seemed to take up all the space. She glanced around. The place was neat, if a bit musty being closed up for so long. But it was nothing to compare with the lavish Holden ranch home.

"Go change into dry clothes," she instructed Joey. He ran into his room. She just hoped he'd pick out something that was suitable, and not a bathing suit with a sweater.

Turning, she brushed back her dripping hair.

"You should go change, too," Mitch suggested.

"I'm fine."

"You'll get chilled if you stay wet. I'm not going anywhere."

It almost sounded ominous.

"What about you?" she said, stalling.

"I doubt you have anything here that will fit me. I'll be fine. I can change when I return to the motel."

She brought him a towel and then went to her room to change. She was nervous, no denying that. Why had Mitch come? She thought she'd explained everything in her note.

He looked so good. She wanted to just fling herself into his arms and let him hold her. But she couldn't do that again. She must never forget that.

Reasonably dry, she returned to the living room. Mitch had taken off his shirt and hung it in the doorway to the kitchen. It was too damp to dry quickly, but he was probably warmer with it off.

She definitely was, unable to stop staring at his broad chest. She'd lain against those warm muscles, trailed her fingers through the light covering of curly hair, rested her cheek on his shoulder.

He held out a rumpled sheet of paper. It was her note.

She looked at him. "I thought it explained everything."

"Now that you know who Joey's father is, are you hoping for some kind of reconciliation?" he asked.

Ginny was dumbfounded. "Of course not!"

How could he ever imagine such a thing? Hadn't she told him over a hundred times over the last week she was in Texas how much she loved him.

And hadn't he been silent every time? She should have listened to that.

"Then you changed your mind about getting married."

She nodded.

"Why?"

"I said in the note."

"That it would be better for us to go our separate ways? Better how?"

"I'm very grateful for what you've done for Joey," she began, but he interrupted.

"Grateful be damned. I don't want your gratitude. I never did."

"But I don't think you wanted my love either, did you? Wasn't I just an obligation you felt saddled with?"

"No."

"I've had a lot of miles to think through. Do you remember asking me to marry you?"

"Of course."

"It was third choice."

"What?"

"It was third choice. First you offered to send me to college, then find me a job. When I didn't take either of those, you came up with marriage."

"I didn't want you to leave."

"And I don't want to live with and compete with a ghost." That would end the discussion. He couldn't come back against that.

"What are you talking about?" He ran his fingers through his hair and stared at her, a frown marring his features.

"I still don't know why you asked me to marry you, but you don't love me. You love Marlisse. You always will. I didn't want to be second best."

He crossed the room in three steps and took her arms in his hands as if holding her lest she try to escape. "You are not now nor ever will be second best. Marlisse is dead. Yes I loved her. A part of me will always love her I expect. Don't you still love your aunt even though she is dead? But I'm not *in* love with a dead woman. I've known that for a while, ever since you came into my life. Didn't you say life moves on? It does. I've been given another chance at the golden ring. Another chance to love a woman who means everything to me, to build a new family, starting with Joey, but hopefully continuing with kids of our own. Marlisse is dead and gone. You are alive, vibrant and enchant me beyond belief. When you left—" he hesitated a long moment, gazing into her eyes. "I knew what it would be like if you never came back. I couldn't deal with it, Ginny. I need you. I want you. You are a part of me."

"You have never once said you loved me," she said simply, almost afraid to believe what he was saying. The facts spoke for themselves. She had trusted a man long ago and been let down. She wasn't sure she was up to it again.

He looked away, as if in pain, releasing her arms, and crossing his own across his chest. Then he faced her again, his eyes wary. "I know. I regret that. I didn't know."

"Know what?"

"Dammit, I didn't know how much I loved you until you left! It was worse than Marlisse's dying. At least her death was an accident, nothing either of us could prevent. And it was over and done with. But your leaving—suddenly I realized what my life would be like without you in it. No bright-eyed optimism, no wide-eyed wonder, no laughter, no loving. It was a damn bleak picture let me tell you. And there wasn't the clean break as with death. You are still alive and so am I. All I could do was plot how to get you back. This time fate wouldn't win. You and I belong together, Ginny. I love you with a love so strong I can't imagine going on if you don't marry me. If you don't spend the rest of the lives we have together with me, I don't know what to do. I can't live in this world and know you are also in it and not with me. Come back. Give me another chance, and I won't blow it this time. I'll tell you every day how much I love you."

Ginny's heart began a heavy beating. Her hopes rose sky high. Tentatively she reached out a hand and rested it on his cool skin. "You really love me?"

"Oh, darling, yes, I love you. More than anything!" He pulled her into his arms and kissed her.

His skin heated, warming her. His muscles bunched and moved as he pulled her closer for a deeper kiss. Her own blood heated, chasing the last of the rain's chill away.

Joey came into the room and stopped when he saw his mother and Mitch kissing. Mitch heard him and slowly ended the kiss, looking over at the small boy.

"Why are you kissing Mommy?" Joey asked.

Mitch held out a hand and Joey came over. Scooping the boy up, Mitch held him in one arm, his other firmly around Ginny. "It's what mommies and daddies do," he said.

"Are you my daddy now?" Joey asked.

"I'm not your biological father, Joey," Mitch said. "But from now on, as long as you live, I'm your Dad."

EPILOGUE

IT WAS a mob scene. The new graduates streamed out into the crowd, looking for relatives and friends. The hot June sunshine beat down causing those in the graduation robes to wish the ceremony had been held in December.

Ginny spotted Mitch, easy to do when he was the tallest man in that direction. She waved and he caught her eye, grinning over the crowd. In only moments he drew near, carrying little Emma, Joey walking proudly by his side. Emaline trailed behind, letting Mitch do the work of making a way through the sea of people. She had worn a frilly pink organdy dress complete with a broad-brimmed Southern belle hat to the ceremonies.

Mitch reached Ginny first. "Congratulations, Ms. College Graduate!" He kissed her. Emma fussed and Ginny reached out to take her in her arms and nuzzle her soft cheek. At two, she was a handful and wanted to get down. Ginny felt her slipping.

"No, you don't," Mitch said taking her back. "We'd lose you in this crowd. You stay with Daddy."

Joey hugged his mom. "I want to go to college and graduate when I get big," he said. At nine, he was almost as tall as his mother. In comparison to Emma, he was so grown up. Ginny kissed his cheek. "And so you shall."

"Goodness, what a crowd!" Emaline said, pushing through and hugging Ginny. "Are you feeling all right? I declare in this heat all I want to do is have a cool lemonade and sit in the shade. You weren't the only pregnant graduate, did you see those other two? I thought that gal with the dark hair might deliver on the stage she is so huge."

Ginny smiled and nodded, resting her hands on the swell of her stomach. Their next child was due in two weeks. She'd known it was cutting it close, and was grateful she had the chance to participate in the graduation ceremonies. It had been a long time in coming.

"Are you ready to head for home?" Mitch asked, his arm around her shoulders, steering her away from the heart of the crowd.

Home. The Holden ranch, where she and Mitch had returned for their August first wedding five years ago. It would always be a magical place to live—because Mitch was there.

He'd adopted Joey shortly after their marriage, explaining to the young boy that his biological father was Mitch's cousin, which that made him and Mitch related by blood, so now Mitch was making it legal, he would always be Joey's dad.

As he was to Emma, their precious baby girl born two years ago. And to the baby she was now carrying.

Mitch had not invited Sammy to family events since discovering his part in Ginny's life. Sammy had given Mitch's name in Florida when on spring break to thumb his nose at his cousin and make sure no one could discover he'd skipped out when he was supposed to be in Texas. He'd gotten a kick out of playing the big honcho like his cousin. Only he would never be the man Mitch Holden was.

Few others in the family knew all the ins and outs, but those that did had welcomed Ginny and Joey with open arms. The others had no reason to hold back. She had the family she had so longed for.

As they settled in the big sedan, Emaline insisted she sit in back with Joey and Emma. Mitch glanced at his wife when they pulled away and slowly moved through the heavy traffic.

"I for one am glad you won't be making the trip into Dallas anymore. I worried every day you did."

She patted his arm and smiled serenely. "I know, but I was careful every time. History won't repeat itself." She knew he still worried about other drivers, fearing something would happen to his second family as it had to his first. Ginny did all she could to allay those fears. Only time would completely heal his fears. And she hoped for another fifty or sixty years at least!

It was amazing, actually, that he loved her so much. In the five years they'd lived together, her own love had grown, as had Mitch's. She had never suspected when knocking on the door in the rain so long ago that life would turn out so happy. Back then, all she'd wanted was the operation for Joey's eyes. Now, she had more happiness than she could ever have hoped for. She had long ago forgiven Sammy. Because of him, she'd found her true love.

He looked at her, meeting her eyes, the knowing reflected in his.

"I can't wait to get you alone," he murmured for her ears alone.

"I'll love that," she replied, her smiled as bright as the Texas sunshine.

HARLEQUIN®
INTRIGUE®

Our unique brand of high-caliber romantic suspense just cannot be contained. And to meet our readers' demands, Harlequin Intrigue is expanding its publishing lineup to include **SIX** breathtaking titles every month!

Here's what we have in store for you:

❑ A trilogy of **Heartskeep** stories by Dani Sinclair

❑ More great **Bachelors at Large** books featuring sexy, single cops

❑ Plus outstanding contributions from your favorite Harlequin Intrigue authors, such as Amanda Stevens, B.J. Daniels and Gayle Wilson

MORE variety.
MORE pulse-pounding excitement.
MORE of your favorite authors and series.
Every month.

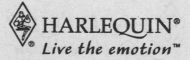

HARLEQUIN®
Live the emotion™

Visit us at www.tryIntrigue.com   HI4T06B

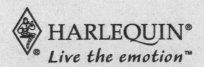

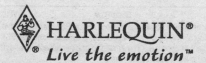

If you enjoyed what you just read,
then we've got an offer you can't resist!

Take 2 bestselling love stories FREE!

Plus get a FREE surprise gift!

Clip this page and mail it to Harlequin Reader Service®

IN U.S.A.
3010 Walden Ave.
P.O. Box 1867
Buffalo, N.Y. 14240-1867

IN CANADA
P.O. Box 609
Fort Erie, Ontario
L2A 5X3

YES! Please send me 2 free Harlequin Romance® novels and my free surprise gift. After receiving them, if I don't wish to receive anymore, I can return the shipping statement marked cancel. If I don't cancel, I will receive 6 brand-new novels every month, before they're available in stores! In the U.S.A., bill me at the bargain price of $3.34 plus 25¢ shipping & handling per book and applicable sales tax, if any*. In Canada, bill me at the bargain price of $3.80 plus 25¢ shipping & handling per book and applicable taxes**. That's the complete price and a savings of 10% off the cover prices—what a great deal! I understand that accepting the 2 free books and gift places me under no obligation ever to buy any books. I can always return a shipment and cancel at any time. Even if I never buy another book from Harlequin, the 2 free books and gift are mine to keep forever.

186 HDN DNTX
386 HDN DNTY

Name	(PLEASE PRINT)	
Address	Apt.#	
City	State/Prov.	Zip/Postal Code

* Terms and prices subject to change without notice. Sales tax applicable in N.Y.
** Canadian residents will be charged applicable provincial taxes and GST.
  All orders subject to approval. Offer limited to one per household and not valid to current Harlequin Romance® subscribers.
  ® are registered trademarks of Harlequin Enterprises Limited.

HROM02   ©2001 Harlequin Enterprises Limited

Georgette Heyer is
"…the next best thing to reading Jane Austen."
—*Publishers Weekly*

GEORGETTE HEYER

POWDER
AND PATCH

Featuring a foreword by
USA TODAY bestselling author
Susan Wiggs

Cleone Charteris is an English belle who yearns for a refined,
aristocratic husband…but ends up loving rogue Phillip Jettan instead!

Available in February 2004.

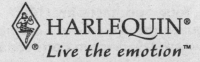

HARLEQUIN®
Live the emotion™

Visit us at www.eHarlequin.com

PHGH602

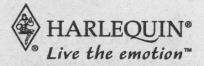

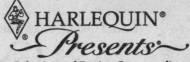
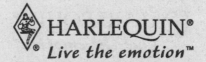